Other Books in The Vintage Library
of Contemporary World Literature

Blood of Requited Love   BY MANUEL PUIG

The Guardian of the Word   BY CAMARA LAYE

History A Novel   BY ELSA MORANTE

A Minor Apocalypse   BY TADEUSZ KONWICKI

We Love Glenda So Much and
A Change of Light   BY JULIO CORTÁZAR

Aké: The Years of Childhood   BY WOLE SOYINKA

Correction   BY THOMAS BERNHARD

Maíra   BY DARCY RIBEIRO

Masks   BY FUMIKO ENCHI

One Day of Life   BY MANLIO ARGUETA

The Questionnaire   BY JIŘÍ GRUŠA

THE
TEN THOUSAND
THINGS

THE
TEN THOUSAND
THINGS

MARIA DERMOÛT

Translated by Hans Koning

AVENTURA

The Vintage Library of Contemporary World Literature

VINTAGE BOOKS   A DIVISION OF RANDOM HOUSE   NEW YORK

CONTENTS

ONE   *The Island*   *1*

TWO   *At the Inner Bay*   *23*
The Small Garden   Himpies

THREE   *At the Outer Bay*   *131*
The Commissioner   Constance and the Sailor
The Professor

FOUR   *The Island*   *225*

When the ten thousand things have been seen in their unity, we return to the beginning and remain where we have always been.

TS'EN SHEN

· ONE ·

THE ISLAND

O N THE ISLAND in the Moluccas there were a few
gardens left from the great days of spice growing
and 'spice parks'—a few only. There had never
been many, and on this island they had even long ago
been called not 'parks' but 'gardens.'

Now, as then, the gardens spread along both bays—
outer bay and inner bay—the spice trees clustered together,
kind with kind, clove with clove, nutmeg with nutmeg;
a few high shade trees in between, kanari trees usually,
and on the bayside coconut palms and plane trees to give
shelter from the wind.

Of all the houses not one was standing whole; they had

collapsed with an earthquake and been cleared away. Here and there a piece of an old house had remained: a wing, a wall only, and later people built against it, usually just a few shabby rooms.

What was left of all the glory?

Yet something seemed to have lingered in those gardens of the old, the past, of the so-very-long-ago.

On a sunny spot between the small trees—when it gets warm there's such a strong smell of spices there . . .

In one of those silent ruined rooms, with a real Dutch sash window and a deep window sill . . .

On a stretch of beach under the planes, where the little waves of the surf flow out: three waves, one behind the other—behind the other—behind the other . . .

What could it be?

The remembrance of a human being, of something that happened, can remain in a place, tangible almost—perhaps there is someone left who knows of it and thinks about it sometimes. Here it was different again: with no foothold anywhere, no certainty—nothing more than a question? a perhaps?

Did two lovers once hold each other here and whisper —forever—or did they let each other go between the little nutmeg trees and say—goodbye?

Did a child play with her doll on the window sill?

Who was standing on the beach then, staring over the three little waves of the surf? and over the bay? at what?

A silence like an answer, a silence of both resignation and expectation; a past and not past.

There was not much else left.

Two of the gardens were haunted.

In a little garden at the outer bay, close to the town, a drowned man walked; but that was of not so long ago, of now, so to speak. And in another garden at the inner bay there were, from far time, three little girls.

The house there was gone: even the foundations and the pieces of wall which had remained standing a long time after the earthquake and fire had finally been cleared away. But a guest pavilion was left, under the trees close to the beach: four large rooms on an open side gallery.

And it was inhabited too: the lady who owned the garden lived in it herself.

She had a beautiful name—Mrs. Von So-and-so (that had been her husband's name; he was from an East Prussian noble family)—and she was the last of an old Dutch line of spicegrowers.

For five generations the garden had been in the family; after her, her son would have been the sixth generation; after him, his children the seventh—but it was not to be like that. Her son had died young and childless and she was an old woman, beyond fifty now, without other children, without other relatives—the last one.

According to the custom of the island, where they had trouble remembering difficult names and where everyone had a byname, she was called 'the lady of the inner bay,' or also 'the lady of the Small Garden,' for that was the name of the garden.

The Small Garden—only in a manner of speaking: it was a large garden, one of the largest on the island, extending at the back far into the hills up to the foot of a steep mountain range, bordered in front by the inner bay, and on the left and right by rivers.

The river to the left, where the land was low and level, flowed brown and sluggish through the trees, not very deep and almost always fordable. But the people from the village on the other shore preferred to cross it on a little raft that they pushed with a bamboo pole.

To the right the hills continued down to the beach; a small wild river bounced foamingly over the rocks, through a valley and so on to the inner bay.

In the valley the poultry was housed, chickens and ducks; the cow sheds were there too—so much clear water at hand to scrub the barns and the runs, and not too close to the house.

Behind the pavilion and at a right angle there was a whole row of annexes—low-ceilinged and with thick stone walls. On one side, in its wooden bell tower, the slave bell still hung; it was rung now for every proa which came or left—welcome . . . goodbye—if someone happened to be at hand. It was also often forgotten.

Behind it the wood began, a lovely wood with many paths and clearings between the trees, especially in this part close to the house. Everything grew there, pell-mell, useful and not useful—spice trees, fruit trees, kanari trees full of nuts, palms: arèn palms from which sugar and syrup were tapped, many coco palms, sago palms in the moist places. But also flowering trees, or rare trees, or trees which were just beautiful.

A small straight lane—going nowhere—of cassowarinas, high firs with long drooping needles, as smooth and straight as the feathers of a cassowary, stirred by every breeze from the inner bay—rustling, lisping, as if they were standing there whispering together. The singing trees they were called.

A water-clear brook ran through the wood; higher up part of it was led through a hollow tree trunk to a stone reservoir marked by a sculptured lion's head with a mossy green mane. From the gaping mouth several spouts of water arched across each other, down into a dug-out stone cistern: a large yet shallow cistern with a wide edge of masonry to sit upon.

All this was in the shade: the cistern, the reservoir with its sculpture, the tree trunks, the ground, all was moist, thickly covered by moss or molded with black and dark-green spots—only the surface of the water held the light in its clarity, in the transparent ripples which swept across it.

It was the old bathing place, shallow for the children, seldom used any more—where were the children? The birds from the wood now came to drink here.

Fat gray wood pigeons, with only their feather collars gleamingly green—the nutpickers—drank there long and carefully, with gurgling sounds, and then roo-kooed, satisfied. A few glittering green parakeets sat together at the edge of the cistern; they were more lost in one another than interested in the water. And sometimes, in a whirl of shouting colors—emerald green, or scarlet, or very gaudy yellow and sky blue and green and red mixed—came a whole flock of loories, or bètès, or whatever their name might be, with hooked yellow beaks like small parrots, and beat their wings, picked fiercely at one another, bathed, drank, splashed in the water, and made an infernal racket

—just for a short moment—then they were gone, and the bathing place was left still and dead between the trees.

Then sometimes in that silence a few hummingbirds descended in an arch of color, skimmed over the surface of the water and rose again, light as feathers—they were never still for a second.

At the edge of the wood, but under the trees, were three children's graves next to each other in the high grass; the tombstones had broken and lost their inscriptions. The names of the children had been Elsbet, Katie and Marregie; the lady of the Small Garden knew that, although all the old papers had been lost in the bad earthquake and fire. They had been the daughters of her great-great-grand-father.

Sometimes the three of them sat on the edge of the cistern in the wood—sh-h-h!

Past the three graves, the path suddenly went steeply up into the hills, hills without many high trees, open and sunny, overgrown with a thick yellowish grass that smelled of herbs, and full of wild rosebushes. And from there, over the tops of the trees, over the house and the out-buildings, she could see the inner bay—like a round blue lake, with here and there light-green discolorings where the water was shallow and dark-green ones where it was very deep, around it the white ridge of the surf and all the luxuriant green of the coast.

Behind the hills, wood again—jungle—dark blue and purple rather than green from a distance; and then the wild mountains.

Up in the mountains the wind always blew.

In the hills the cows of the lady of the Small Garden were tended and the deer grazed.

Sometimes the three little girls played there in the afternoon sun, if there was no one about—'there were rose leaves lying everywhere again!' the cowherd said, 'oh, let them be,' the lady of the Small Garden replied.

And sometimes, not often, they crouched next to each other on the beach of the bay, under the planes, away from the house, to see what kinds of shells had been washed ashore. They dug into the sand (that could clearly be seen later). Those shells do hide themselves . . .

All the people knew the three girls and watched for them. They did not want to scare them off, and as long as they looked the other way and pretended not to see them the girls went on playing peacefully—so the people said. The lady of the Small Garden had never seen the three girls, she was sorry about that.

Was seeing necessary? As long as she could remember, she had heard about them; they belonged, they had a fixed place in her garden on the island in the Moluccas, and also in her own life.

The lady of the Small Garden sometimes had the feeling that the island lay before her, as if on a map, to look at—complete with compass card drawn in one corner.

It was a mountainous island—the few level stretches along the coasts were strewn with fantastically shaped rocks. Trees everywhere, even in the water; at the bay, beside the swamp covered with lilac water hyacinths, were rows of gleaming little nipa palms and somber mangrove trees on their tortured bare trunks. Sometimes there were sea snails on the branches, under convex white shells, like porcelain fruit.

So much clear water everywhere—fresh water—rivers, wells, brooks, cascades over the rocks.

There was a net of roads and paths and tracks and stairs hewn in the mountains, leading to large and small villages: of Christians, of Mohammedans; the old communities under the mystic numbers Nine and Five (Nine and Five do not tolerate each other at all). In between, here and there, a 'garden,' a decrepit little fort, a small old church with seventeenth-century Dutch armorial shields, a gaudily painted wooden mosque beside its tall minaret, a large carved tombstone over a forgotten grave—In Everlasting Remembrance—everlasting is so long! And the one large town on the outer bay.

She knew the island so well, up to the steepest mountain, down into the deepest jungle; she had sailed all the coasts in a proa. She knew where, here and there and everywhere, a never-seen tree or plant grew, a strange flower bloomed. She had so often leaned over the edge of her proa to look through a hollow bamboo at the sea gardens in the outer bay—the dream vision petrified in the coral, so unreally quiet, in which only a few gaily colored little fish moved as swift as arrows, or tiny brown sea horses hung perpendicularly in the water, staring earnestly at each other. Somewhere there was also a place with nothing but the rare red coral, like a field of red clover under the blue waves.

And she had stood in the woods, high up in the mountains behind the Small Garden, where the little spring spurted which was connected with the sea—how else could the water taste so bitter in the mouth? There prayers for rain were said during great droughts, and sacrifices were made—but nobody was allowed to know of that.

And the people!

The lady of the Small Garden did not know all the people on the island—of course not—but she did know many: an old rajah family with a Portuguese name, and another one, and another; that priest over there, a Moslem, who knew all the stories of the 'holy wars' and 'the heroes of the faith' (fighting had been going on forever on the island, and he himself was a real warrior); Christian religious teachers, some of them great preachers; a poet-singer, a dance leader, a wise woman—a bibi—who could heal and make sick, lay a spell, exorcise ghosts.

In the town the Dutch, bustling around, busily coming and going. Only a few who stayed; a few who were buried and so stayed forever.

And travelers from all over the world came to the Moluccas, travelers who, immediately off the boat—quickly, quickly, quickly—wanted to buy shells, coral, pearls which weren't there, butterflies, old china, orchids, birds; in the end they were content with a little basket of nutmeg branches with flowers and leaves made of parakeet feathers—poor creatures—and there they were, back at the ship's railing, forgetting to wave. Strange people!

Everywhere there are strange people; on the island too. They had shown her an empty hut at the bay, where not so long ago had lived a man and a boy who in reality were a shark and a little shark; those two had never laughed, so as not to show their pointed teeth. Now they had gone! Where? They were certainly swimming together in the bay.

And if she were only patient she might yet see the old woman, the mother of the Pox. In houses with children there was always a branch with thorns tied against the front door, to keep her out; she couldn't do much harm from a distance. She had not often been seen in recent years.

But the lady frequently met the man who was called 'the man with the blue hair.' He was just a simple fisher from the village next to the Small Garden, a man who regularly dyed his gray curly head a clear blue with indigo. He had to do it: his only son was a soldier somewhere far away, a hero! In the moonlight the young men of the villages sang songs about him; named his battles, the fortifications he had stormed, his victories, his wounds—and such a hero would have for a father a toothless old man with white hair? Impossible!

Sometimes the lady of the Small Garden listened to the island: how the bays rustled, the inner bay differently from the outer bay, and the open sea beyond still different again. That was the land wind sighing, and that the sea wind, and that the howl of the storm wind which is called Baratdaja.

Thus sounded the drums, giving the proa rowers their rhythm; that was the light, clattering sound of the strings of empty mussel shells bound to the mast or the bow to lure the wind which liked to come and play with them; and that was the short reverberating thud with which a proa went about, from one wing onto the other.

Those who were musical remembered the melodies of all songs, all dances; here they still used the small copper cymbals of Ceram, the 'land at the other side'; there they blew on the Triton shells, which are shining orange inside; and once she had made a long trip to hear someone sing the 'song of the dying fishes' as only that man could sing it.

And the familiar sounds: the voices of people and children and animals; music, songs of every day from the village across the river, from the garden.

Someone sang a love song in the moonlight: 'the evening is too long, beloved, and the road too far'—others clapped their hands with it—a single bamboo flute, languishing.

A lullaby for a child, or a story sung to it, battle songs of the wild Alfuras, head-hunters of Ceram. And sometimes, very rarely, the old heathen lament (careful, don't let the schoolteacher hear it) for one who has just died. 'The hundred things' was the name of the lament—the hundred things of which the dead one is reminded, which are asked him, told him.

Not only the people in his life: this girl, this woman and that one, that child, your father, your mother, a brother or sister, the grandparents, a grandchild, a friend, a comrade-in-arms; or his possessions: your beautiful house, your china dishes hidden in the attic, the swift proa, your sharp knife, the little inlaid shield from long ago, the two silver rings on your right hand, on index finger and thumb, the tamed pigeon; but also: hear, how the wind blows!—how white-crested the waves come running from the high sea!—the fishes jump out of the water and play with each other—look how the shells gleam on the beach—remember the coral gardens under water, and how they are colored—and the bay!—the bay!—please never forget the bay! And then they said: oh soul of so-and-so, and ended with a long-held melancholy *ee-ee-ee? ee-ee-ee?* over the water.

Or she listened with the others to the hammering from just across the bay, from the place where formerly the Portuguese wharf had stood (the beautiful galleons with all the woodwork were once calked there, and occasionally a gibbet must have been built there too)—now there were only trees; and the knocking of a wooden hammer on a wooden beam, heard clearly over the water—could that be a bird?

And whenever a proa came or went, the old slave bell in the Small Garden was rung—if someone were there to do it.

These were many things, but not all, and not enough. There remained the imagined things, figures as they were depicted in dances and in songs and stories; inventions— nothing more—how could she name them all?

At the inner bay only:

Right at the corner, where the bay is narrowest and at its deepest from the suction of the tide, every now and

again a sailor walked on the cliff, a young Portuguese who
had drowned there; he had wanted to go home, he had
heard his name called far away, Martin was his name.

Or Martha, the young daughter of the rajah of a village which no longer existed, who tried to cross the water
on her little horse in the moonlit night—to her lover, a
poor fisherman who had no proa, and her father had ordered all the proas of the village bound up high on the
shore. She always reached the other side—she never
reached the other side . . .

Under the cliff, in a hollow in the rocks, the octopus
was waiting, not a little one like so many which swim in
the bay but the gigantic Octopus—the One—with all its
eight terrible wriggling grasping arms full of sucking cups,
glaring out of two black bulging little eyes. It saw everything, because it could see in the light and it could see
in the dark; but no one could see the Octopus. Every
fisher, every rower knew about it, every helmsman watched
carefully at that corner.

Farther down the great purple swamp, and an isthmus
from which often came the labored singing of men hauling
their proas across it.

Still farther down that way was the village next to the
Small Garden, and there lived 'the man with the blue
hair' and also the woman who led 'the dance of the Shell.'
One time, it was already long ago, the lady of the Small
Garden had seen it—strictly speaking it wasn't allowed.
Nowadays that dance was not danced any more, neither in
the village across the river nor anywhere else.

Next to the village, in the Small Garden, those three
little girls who had all died on the same day—that must

have been with the bad earthquake and the fire? No! It was not with the earthquake and the fire.

And the coral woman.

She would certainly not forget the coral woman; as a matter of fact one could read all about her in Mr. Rumphius's books: just beyond the garden there had been a small colony of Javanese, not more than one large family. When the proa in which they had first come anchored, a young woman had bent over its edge to look into the water at the coral plants of the depth—perhaps she was looking for the Tree, the Coco Palm of the Sea, which is of course also of coral.

She bent over too far and fell with her head forward into the water, and did not come back up—until, much later, the coral fishers found a large block of coral there in the shape of a woman. It was she, the Javanese! No mistake possible. Her head was embedded in the coral, and when they loosened her she groaned—the coral fishers said.

After that she stood for years in the garden of Mr. Rumphius, who had bought her for five rix-dollars. He put some leaf mold in the little holes in the coral, and seeds of dwarf climbers, and in due time the coral woman had a nice flowery dress to cover her nudity.

Did he ever walk up to her and look at her with his almost blind eyes, in the evening when all has become quiet, dark and light under the stars, and did he ask her— whether?

For Mr. Rumphius also believed in the Coco Palm of the Sea: the coconuts which are washed ashore now here, then there, have to come from somewhere, don't they?

So different from an ordinary coconut, almost twice as large, not round but oblong; polished by waves and surf, almost black, hard as stone.

Not on this island, on none of the 'thousand islands,' nor on the large islands far away, nor on the continents either, grew a coco palm with such fruits. What he had been able to find out about it he had written down: there were those who said the palm obviously did not grow on land but in the sea, in a whirlpool in the 'navel of the seas'—he could not believe that. More likely in a quiet, secluded spot—but in deep water, he thought, in a bay, a bay like the inner bay, for instance.

The palm would have a black trunk and black branches (the small coral trees had those too); black ribbon-shaped leaves like an ordinary coco palm? Of that he wasn't sure —as a matter of fact, under the water black isn't always black, sometimes it is between purple and violet, sometimes lilac. There were moreover a Crab and a Bird who belonged with the palm; coral fishers had seen them, but they had never been able to get close to them.

Did Mr. Rumphius ask the coral woman whether she —perhaps—while she was down there—?

He wanted so desperately much to see the Coco Palm of the Sea—black, or purple, or red as a rose (with the Crab and the Bird)—just once before he would be totally blind; that couldn't be far off any more.

What did the coral woman, what did her closed coral mouth answer him?

The lady of the Small Garden liked her so much because she liked Mr. Rumphius so much. Both his works had always been in the house at the Small Garden: with her grandmother she had looked up plants and medicinal herbs in one of the many volumes of the *Herb Book,* and in his *Book of Curiosities* the names of 'shells and horns and snails and jellyfish and other such little fellows.'

She herself belonged to the island too—here, in her garden at the inner bay, in front of the guest pavilion, under the planes, the little waves of the surf at her feet.

Everyone knew how she looked: small and bent, in her sarong and simple white cotton jacket with the smallest of lace edges or no lace at all and no beautiful brooch, just held together with safety pins; in bare feet on strong leather sandals, full of freckles, always bareheaded, with springy graying hair.

They had seen her or they had heard about her. Everywhere on the island they talked about her, whispered sometimes—as before about her grandmother, and before that about the grandmother of her grandmother (there was not much to talk or to whisper about the men in the family).

They didn't speak evil of her; why should they?

They liked her. Now at least, once they had not; she was a terribly bossy woman who always wanted to know everything very precisely but who was prepared to help when help was needed, or sympathy.

She herself had been grievously tried in life: her grandmother dead, to whom she owed everything; both her parents—they had never cared much about her; brothers and sisters she did not have; her husband—nobody knew the real story of that husband: 'A big man,' they said, but no one knew him, he had never been on the island, he must have died years and years ago; and now not so long ago her son too, her only child.

So she had no one left.

But there was one matter in which she went too far.

One day, one night in the year, on the day her son had died, she wanted to be alone—that was acceptable, but she went to such lengths that she even sent away all the servants with their families, to the town at the outer bay. She would not receive visitors on that day either; when people came all the same—absolutely not from curiosity but to cheer her up—she asked them to postpone their visit to some other time, and quietly let them go back the whole way again, no matter who they were.

One day, one night a year dedicated to the dead? Is even that too much?

But it wasn't like that! She did not dedicate that day and that night to the dead, but only to those who had been murdered, murdered on the island.

Not every year was there a murder, luckily not! Years could pass without one. It was a peaceful island, and yet, it could happen . . .

As in that certain year when there had been four. Four? Or was it three? But three certainly; in one case it wasn't clear whether the man had been murdered or not, but drowned in the bay he surely was.

Not much happened on the island that the lady of the Small Garden did not hear of; and when a murder had been committed she immediately went to inquire, and

wanted to know how or what? where it had happened?
who had been murdered? who had done it? why? with
what—but she didn't care so much about that; it was no
morbid curiosity in her, she didn't think she had to clear
up something—that was for the police. She pitied the
murdered one and the relatives; she would have liked to
understand what had led to it, help somehow if possible
—but usually it was not possible.

Still she could commemorate the murdered on that one
day in the year. She didn't arrange flowers or light candles
for them or such fiddle-faddle; she didn't burn incense, she
had never liked incense—commemorate, only and simply
commemorate.

She had started it after the death of her son. About
that she never spoke any more, as she sometimes had in
the beginning; her son had been murdered, at least that
was what she thought.

Some people took it amiss: the young officers in the garrison of the town at the outer bay said that it was time
someone made her understand: her son, also an officer
—a comrade-in-arms—had fallen. Not fallen in open com-
bat, true—shot down from an ambush; but shooting from
an ambush is not forbidden in battle—honestly fallen! And
so one shouldn't talk about murder.

But the lady of the Small Garden never spoke to the
officers about his being murdered; and when they saw her,
the young men did not say anything about honest battles.

Some of the older people who might have heard about
'certain kinds of things' whispered that perhaps she had
secret powers—was that why she wanted to be completely
alone?—but no one knew whether she did 'certain kinds

of things.' She never sent for one of those wise women to exorcise ghosts from the garden, as happened when her grandmother was still alive.

Her grandmother! Yes, that one—that was a different story—she had certainly had secret powers, you can be sure of it! But the lady of the Small Garden did not; otherwise she would really have been able to see the three ghost girls in her own garden—every fisherman's child has seen them.

All these things, and still others, and with the sky added, were the island.

· TWO ·

AT THE INNER BAY

THE SMALL GARDEN

· I ·

THE GIRL was born at the Small Garden and her mother wanted her to be named Felicia. The father agreed, he always agreed to everything. The grandmother did not agree at all. 'Happy! You dare to call your little child Happy! How do you know in advance?'

But the mother had insisted.

The grandmother would never call her that way; she always said 'granddaughter,' and from then on the parents were 'son' and 'daughter-in-law.' 'Granddaughter' and 'son' were friendly words, 'daughter-in-law' was not.

The child spent the first seven, almost eight years of her

life on the island in the Moluccas; the family had another house in the town at the outer bay and it was there that she lived with her parents. Her mother had refused to stay at the Small Garden, and her mother always did everything she wanted and never did anything she did not want; she could because she had all the money. Her mother owned a sugar plantation on Java, something quite different from a little nothing of a spice garden on an island in the Moluccas.

Felicia's father often went to the Garden, almost every week; sometimes Felicia and her nurse were allowed to come along.

It was impossible to think of anything more wonderful than a stay at the Small Garden on the inner bay.

First, the trip there in a proa; you walked along the path behind the fort, the Castle—and there under an awning at the quay lay her grandmother's proa, waiting to take them to the Garden.

When they arrived at the Garden a bell was rung.

At high tide the proa could moor at a stone embankment in the inner bay, at low tide the rowers carried them ashore one by one, in a chair; sometimes one of the rowers lifted Felicia out of the proa and onto his shoulders in one swoop, rowers are terribly strong!

And later the fishermen from the village across the river might take her and her nurse out to sea, usually in a winged proa which could be sailed. If the wind did not rise, the fishers whistled and asked, wouldn't Mister Wind come and loosen his long hair? They sang and laughed and talked, and teased Susanna the nurse because she had such fat arms and legs.

At the Garden she could walk a little way into the sea—
Susanna watched out for sea urchins—or look for shells
on the beach under the plane trees, or bathe in the cistern
in the wood. She could help pick fruit in the orchard of the
lemon trees: between the small lemon bushes stood some
larger ones, grapefruit, one with red pulp. 'That is your
tree, granddaughter,' the grandmother said, 'because you
like the fruit so much. You are right: the red is much
sweeter than the white.' She could pick kanari nuts in the
wood, or listen to the 'singing trees.'

But in the wood there also lived the palm-wine mannikin.

When one of the high arèn palms was going to be
tapped, they hung a little fellow in the tree to watch for
thieves. He was cut from rough wood, about two feet long,
dressed in old rags, with a mustache and a curly head of
black palm hairs, a fiery red mouth, black-and-white gleaming eyes; and right through him they stuck a black rattan
thorn, almost as long as he was himself and as thick as a
finger, with the needle-sharp point sticking out in front.

Up there in the high palm tree the little fellow couldn't
do much harm, but at times he climbed down the small
rattan ladder, quick as a monkey, and pursued someone
with his thorn! then you had to watch out, and hide fast.

Susanna the nanny always watched carefully for the
mannikin, but Felicia did not have much confidence in
Susanna.

Then again they might go for a walk with the cowherd
—all was safe with him—through the wood and farther
out into the hills; perhaps they would see a wild deer.
Felicia thought that she wouldn't be afraid of a wild deer,

not even up close, but of the cows she was scared even from a distance. And alone with Susanna she went to the green, the quiet valley where it was never quiet because of the cackling of the chickens and the chatter of the ducks. She did not care much for the chickens—they ran away when someone waved his arms and cried *ssst*—but she detested the ducks.

Ducks were false through and through. Not as long as they swam around in the stream and dived and chattered together—but when they waddled ashore, they changed into awkward, cruel creatures that followed and swallowed everything that couldn't get away fast enough, especially the beautiful duck crabs.

Susanna had put one in her hand to look at: a smooth blinking little shield, not bigger than a penny, eight bright red legs, two miniature claws, one on each side. These poor crabs immediately admitted defeat, rolled themselves into little balls, pulled in their tender red legs and claws and let themselves be swallowed—alive—by the ducks.

'They are good little crabs,' Susanna stated. 'They never do any harm, they just sit quietly in the bellies of the ducks; and when they put out a leg and tickle them, the ducks like that so much that they go and lay an egg; but watch out when the ducks swallow those dark-brown crabs, their stomachs get cut to pieces.'

'Do the ducks die from that?' asked Felicia, who wanted nothing better.

Of course they did!

It seemed to Felicia that the ducks must eat only the beautiful brown-and-red crabs; there were never any fewer of them, and they were certainly very alive and healthy.

But all this was child's play compared with the other thing, the bad, the really bad. Over in the valley near the river there was a large white open shell from which the chickens drank their water, and in that shell the beast had lived, lived still—the Leviathan, Susanna said.

Susanna the nanny had a disease which had made her arms and legs swell and look like tightly stuffed brown sausages to which the hands and feet were tied; yet her shapeless wrists and ankles had remained supple, and she was quick enough in her movements. The disease was not contagious, the doctor said.

Felicia did not know quite what to think of her: it wasn't only those fat arms and legs—she could behave so strangely on occasion. She was always taking Felicia some place where there were no other people—she did this at home, in the town at the outer bay, and also on the Small Garden—in order to recite her psalms without being disturbed.

She was very pious, knew her psalms and recited them in Malayan with a ringing voice, and she taught them to Felicia at the same time. Felicia was at the age when a child learns things by heart easily even without understanding their meaning.

Susanna had one favorite psalm: the hundred and fourth. Felicia could say large parts of Psalm 104 in Malayan without stumbling. Yet it was a difficult psalm, full of the names of animals she did not know: the wild donkeys, the storks in the pine trees—a stork was the bird Lakh-lakh—the high mountains of the wild goats, the rocks for the rabbits, and the roaring young lions—a lion's name was Singa—and then the sea with its wriggling beasts, large and small, and the ships, and the Leviathan who is too terrible!

That was the same Leviathan who lived—here—in the shell under the trees, in the green valley of the Small Garden.

It was a gigantically large shell, more than three feet in diameter, covered with a rough chalky growth on the outside, deeply carved, the edge crenated, the inside a smooth ivory white—and that was only half of it. No one knew where the other half had gone.

Once there had been two equal shells which fitted exactly onto each other, unbreakably linked at one place: only the beast that lived inside was strong enough to open and close those two lead-heavy shells just as it pleased.

Susanna showed her how it had been: her heavy wrists carefully pressed against each other, she held her fat brown hands as if they were shells, the fingertips closed together; and with a jerk she opened, closed, opened the two shells. She had so much strength in her hands that her fingers made a thud when they came together.

'Like this!' she said. Like this!'

And then she began the description of the beast that had grown inside the shell. It was gruesome to behold: thick and shapeless like a big full bag, a leathery skin, spotted and striped like a snake—but different again: white with brown and black and also dark blue; and it was blind!

'No eyes,' Susanna whispered, and squeezed her own eyes.

Felicia did not know why, but that was the most horrid part of it all.

A mouth it did have, and it could eat, or at least suck. The shells had not been lying on the ground, clearly visible; no, under water, on the bottom of the bay where it was not too deep, hidden between the coral, and overgrown with algae and seaweed.

First the beast opened the two shells—carefully—just a crack, and then a little bit more, and still a bit more, and it waited motionlessly, Susanna said, until someone came —a coral diver or a fisher—and then Felicia had to put a hand or a foot in the shell, whether she wanted to or not.

'Like this!' said Susanna, and like lightning the edge of her hand came down on Felicia's arm or leg where it rested on that crenated edge of the shell, 'like this! clear off! and look at all the blood!'

The child stood petrified—the two shells were closed, and her hand was cut off and lying inside and the beast was starting to eat it. It hurt terribly, and she didn't know where to go with the bleeding stump.

'He sucks on it, he likes it,' Susanna stated; but when it became too much for Felicia, who started to sniffle, she tried to console her, 'don't cry, he doesn't always eat hands or feet, oh no, fish too, he catches them in his shell, and he has a friend, a shrimp, only as big as a finger—a finger of yours—who lives with him in the shell. The shrimp shares in the food but he has to help with the catch: he tells the beast when to open the shell wider and when to close it; the beast can't see, you know that, no eyes!'

Susanna paused for Felicia to ask, does he have ears? Can the shrimp talk with him? But after the first time she refused to ask that—Susanna had to tell it herself, that the Leviathan could not hear because he had no ears, 'no

31

eyes, you know that, and no ears,' but the shrimp had a little claw and pinched the beast with it in his leathery skin: then he knew what to do, open the shells or close them.

Susanna made a sharp shrimp's claw with her fat index finger and thumb, the nails against each other, and pinched Felicia in her arm, a piece of skin between the nails.

'Like this,' Susanna said.

Felicia screamed: it hurt much more than the snapping off of a hand or foot! She would have liked to slap the maid; she had at times but it never worked out well, what with those strong heavy hands of Susanna's. She swallowed and tried hard not to cry; her grandmother always saw it afterward when she had cried, and wanted to know why, and then said: 'You must learn to be a proud girl, granddaughter, upright, and not to cry about small things.'

She did not like to hear that—she didn't cry about small things, but obviously she couldn't tell her grandmother about the Leviathan.

The grandmother was a skinny little woman with a dark complexion, dark hair and dark eyes. She herself always walked very upright in her neat clothes: usually a bright silk sarong from Timor or one of the other islands, a jacket of thin white batiste with broad lace, a single jewel—a golden pin in her hair knot—around each wrist a bracelet of black coral like a bent twig—against rheumatism—on one hand two wedding rings, her own and that of her husband who had died so young. Her slippers were of velvet embroidered with gold thread and spangles; she embroidered the velvet herself and the Chinese shoe-maker in the town at the outer bay had to make slippers out of it.

She also sewed the fine jackets herself; and she made amber balls and scents and medicines. She began by weigh-ing herbs and roots on a little scale, or by cutting off pieces of them—as long as a finger, as long as the nail of her forefinger—scraped them clean and ground them to a powder in a wooden or china mortar—never, never in a metal one—sometimes they were cooked and then strained through a cloth; sometimes brewed like tea—always with rain water, remember that!

Felicia felt a holy awe for her grandmother's medicines; luckily most of them were not meant for children and she was never ill; but there was a draught of a brightly orange root—for the purification of the blood after the change of the monsoon—no one, old or young, escaped that. It was as bitter as bile. And of course once a month castor oil, if she had not already taken it at home—with coffee extract or anisette, she could take her pick.

The grandmother also cooked well and made preserves: pickles, jams, mussel sauce (black or white), kanari cakes. She did everything herself and at home, with two old servants who had been there a long time.

Everything in the house had been 'a long time'; also the things in the 'special drawer' of her cabinet.

It was an antique cabinet full of cracks and crevices, on a base with bent legs, the front ones ending in claws; both its doors had to be opened before the drawer could be pulled out.

On the shelves above it were little stacks of clothes, sarongs, jackets, underwear, and then neat piles of boxes and baskets with herbs and roots and scents—there was such a strong smell of all of them mixed, but the smell of incense dominated. Every now and again the grandmother brought an iron pot from the kitchen holding pieces of glowing charcoal, put it in the opened drawer and sprinkled some grains of incense into it. It was real Arabian incense, yellow like rosin, and transparent, 'congealed tears of Mohammed the prophet, look!' she said. Felicia looked, she didn't know exactly who Mohammed was.

A thin cloud of smoke trailed upward; and the sweetish intoxicating smell was never quite blown out of the room, not even with all the doors opened and the cool wind from the inner bay going through it all day. The cabinet, and the 'special drawer,' were saturated with it.

The bottom of the drawer was neatly covered with sheets of rice paper and against the back was propped a piece of old colored Palembang silk such as they wear in the court of the Sultan, which is a cure for sore throat— a little strip around the neck is sufficient.

On one side of the drawer, a pretty fan of real tortoise, worked in open patterns, with real gold inlay, 'from when we were young,' grandma said, 'each of us five had a fan when we went to a dance in the town or at one of the gardens.'

There had been five sisters, no brothers, nothing but girls! 'We had tiffs, but then we made peace again. It was very gay at the Small Garden, granddaughter. We had dances behind the house, on the spice platform, with

Chinese lanterns in the trees. It did not take each of us very long to find a beau, a beau is a little boy friend,' she said, 'oh, we were all five nice and pretty girls (if I say so myself) and married and gone in a jiffy.'

She had moved to Java with her husband; he had a job with the Customs; and soon she had become a widow and had returned with her little son Willem (one of his grandfather's names had been Willem)—she had returned and stayed—'yes, granddaughter, that is the way things sometimes work out.' Her son Willem was Felicia's father.

The other sisters had never come back, none of them: three were dead now, one lived far away in North America.

At the other end of the drawer stood a basket from Macassar, woven from orchid roots; in it grandma kept her 'jewels.' She didn't own many; there were the gold pins she wore, and then some brooches, a pendant on a chain, a beautiful shell with a silver edge, an amethyst, a little cat's-eye for dreams, and a gold apple, carved out in fretwork, with a ball of amber inside which she had made herself. She unscrewed the fruit and rolled the ball in her hand to warm it, 'sniff, how lovely it smells!' Felicia didn't think it was so lovely, but she didn't dare say so; the ball was put back in the fruit, the basket was closed and put away: it was pretty but it was not the treasure.

The treasure was lying in the middle of the drawer and it consisted of three things: a plate, and two little boxes made of chips of white wood.

A little plate of rough china, glazed a light, even green —a real poison plate from Ceram.

'It warns against poison,' the grandmother said. Poison scared the plate and made it change color, bad poison would make cracks in it, and a really bad poison could make it break right in two.

Once Felicia had asked what poison was.

'Poison, that is the same as venom—Venom,' the grandmother said, pronouncing the 'V' very sharply.

After that Felicia did not ask further: Venom, she realized, had to be something frightening, not a thing to ask or talk or even think about.

On the plate lay the two boxes.

In one, carefully wrapped in a piece of cloth, a 'snakestone' was kept. It was tricky to keep the snakestones straight, there were so many kinds. There were little white stones which snakes sucked on to quench their thirst; then there was the Carbuncle stone which a certain kind of snake wore in its forehead and which gave a red glow in the dark, but that was a very rare one. You couldn't kill the snake to get it, because then the glow of the stone vanished immediately and forever. Occasionally the snake left the stone somewhere as a gift; and when it went to drink or bathe it took it out—the stone must not get wet. That was your opportunity to find it and keep it. But it was no use to anybody else: the Carbuncle stone could not be traded, bought or sold, for then again the glow would vanish. Find it yourself, or get it as a gift.

Felicia's grandmother had until now never found a Carbuncle stone, and no one had ever given her one 'free as a gift for nothing to keep,' she said, 'it is a pity, granddaughter.'

Her snakestone was of quite a different sort. It cured snakebite and the bite of poisonous animals, fishes, scorpions and spiders. The stone sucked the—Venom—out of the wound. Later she would show Felicia how to use it.

The second box was lined with little pieces of blue velvet and in it another stone was lying. It looked like a common white pebble with a bit of a pearly shine over it; and next to it lay a little stone, like a piece broken off the other one. But that was something one should not think and certainly never say!

The very small stone was the child of the other stone. First it had not been there: the larger one had been 'all alone' in the box—and one morning the child was lying next to it, 'born in the night,' grandmother said, and put the top back on the box.

And then there were always some shells in the drawer, nothing special, the kind that grew on the rocks near the bay. The small creatures which made their houses in them were still alive; they were not fed, yet they went on living for months and now and then they moved about with a slight crackling of their shells' edges against the rough paper.

They were there to guard the treasure; grandmother was always careful to get some new ones from the beach regularly. As long as the treasure was guarded by living sentinels no thief would dare touch it, and as long as the treasure was lying in the drawer the house of the Small Garden would be protected against misfortune, and disease, and poverty, and venom, and other unmentionable things; and all who lived there would be—happy, grandmother would never say—not too unhappy, the Lord willing . . .

If she would ever find the Carbuncle stone, or get it as a present—free as a gift for nothing to keep—and (she hardly dared speak the words) the Green Bracelet!—then she would have a treasure of Five.

Five! Five is such a very good number; but that would most likely never happen.

Now it was Three, and three is a lot too. A person must be content with what's given, and manage with that as well as possible; and then she said again, 'you must learn to be a proud girl, upright, and not cry or be scared,' and 'if we can only remain proud people!'

Later Felicia understood that with proud she meant courageous; at least that is what she thought.

And Felicia remembered how it had come about that they had left the island, and how the three girls had been mentioned on that occasion. She had never heard talk of them before, although she had often enough passed the three graves at the edge of the wood. Susanna had never told her about them, but then she did not really belong to the Small Garden.

It all started with the quarrel about the old spicegrower's house, of which the brick foundations and some pieces of wall remained standing, between the trees to the right of the pavilion. Felicia's mother had had a little plan, she always had plans—she wanted to rebuild the house.

It had been a stone house with a second story, not over the whole house but only in front—the Hall—with a row of tall windows with balustrades at the bayside. That second story would not be rebuilt, of course not; everyone knew better now with all those earthquakes: the Hall would be on the ground floor, again with French windows.

Again with wrought-iron balustrades with curlicues and a bit of gilding, and in front a large flower bed, and through the trees the beautiful view on the inner bay.

The view was already there.

The Hall, that was the main thing! The rest of the house wasn't too important. Felicia's mother didn't intend to live there, certainly not; but she had started to look around for old furniture, and chandeliers. She had found a large lamp dating from the eighteen-ten's: two milk-glass bells on top of each other, with glass chains and crystal pendants, and two crystal wall chandeliers. A white marble floor as there had been once, no, that would not do, dark-red tiles, she had thought, and the woodwork a reddish-brown, varnished (the way the Chinese sometimes have it), with here and there a touch of gold; the walls chalked an even white, antique furniture, not too much, a few good pieces. Perhaps grandmother would have her dresser refurbished, and the old chairs around the dining table.

As soon as the Hall was ready she would give a party with candlelight and music; and she wanted all the guests to come in ceremonial proas, illuminated, with the gongs and drums beating—that would sound so wonderful over the inner bay.

She had even made the trip to the Small Garden to ask the grandmother for her permission.

And grandmother has said no—without any ado, just no, no!—to Felicia's mother.

'But for heaven's sake, why not?'

'You know, daughter-in-law. Because it is a house of ill fortune.'

At first grandmother refused to say more, but when the other insisted she went on, 'Why do you pretend not to know these things, that the three little girls of our family died in that house—all three on one day—and have you forgotten also that the house collapsed in the earthquake and that the great-grandmother of your husband was up in the Hall with another child, and that they were buried under the ruins, and that afterward the house burned down? Don't you know all those things?'

'Oh my,' Felicia's mother had said, 'but that's all so long ago!'

'Long ago or not makes no difference: misfortune remains misfortune, daughter-in-law!'

'Well—' the other shrugged— 'I don't believe in that sort of thing. Now you give your permission so that they can start building right away. You will see how beautiful it is all going to be and,' she said, 'of course I'll pay for everything, it won't cost you a penny!'

The grandmother straightened herself even more than usual; she waited a moment before answering, looked out to the spot where the old house had been, 'it is already beautiful here,' she said, 'and you are a fool, daughter-in-law. You have everything to learn—money, I know money is needed if something is to be bought, but you cannot buy happiness with it, nor keep away misfortune. So much the worse for you, daughter-in-law.' She was really angry now, 'and you haven't learned your manners too well: in our family—not on Java, so elegant on the sugar plantation, oh no, right here—with us, with all the sisters at the Small Garden on the inner bay, we learned not to make remarks about pennies!'

That was bad too, for the spicegrowers of the Small Garden on the island in the Moluccas were of a much older family than the owners of the large sugar plantation on Java. And so Felicia's mother had also become angry, so angry that she said she would never put foot again in the Small Garden, and she was not going to stay in that miserable little town at the outer bay either—not another day (she always said that), not she, nor her husband, nor her daughter Felicia!

And thus all three of them had soon thereafter sailed for Europe. And Felicia wouldn't forget the goodbye, for it was then that she had received the Snake with the Carbuncle stone as a present.

In the end her mother had gone with them to the Garden to say goodbye: it was better to part in peace, she had thought. Before they all went back in the proa the grandmother had taken the child to her room, alone, without the parents. She watched her attentively for a short moment, took her hand, 'goodbye, granddaughter,' she said, 'when you come back I'll be here, I will wait for you. You must say that aloud once, so as not to forget—my grandma is waiting for me at the Small Garden on the inner bay.'

Felicia repeated it, although it had given her the shivers to say such a thing aloud. And then grandmother opened her cabinet, not the 'special drawer,' and from behind a little pile of sarongs she brought out a round apothecary's box with a bracelet, which Felicia had never seen before, 'for the return voyage,' she said.

It was a wonderful bracelet, Felicia thought: a golden snake full of rubies; not only the eyes, but the back and the tail too, right down to the tip, were inlaid with them; and it was bent in a spiral.

'Oh,' she said, 'how beautiful! the Snake with the Carbuncle stone; so you did get one after all, grandma,' with a bit of a reproach in her voice—why had she never shown it before?

'A fool you are, granddaughter,' said the grandmother, 'of course this isn't the Snake with the Carbuncle stone! This one is made of gold, the other is alive—that is not the same,' and taking the child by one hand and holding the box with the bracelet in the other, she went out again.

Once more, for the last time, they sat under the planes at the inner bay and drank homemade vanilla lemonade with lemon (from the Garden) and ate a piece of her kanari cake.

'Dear son, daughter-in-law,' the grandmother had said, 'this bracelet is a present of mine to my sweet granddaughter for her voyage back.' Felicia's parents looked at each other—what was that? back? they had not even left yet.

'She is not allowed to wear the bracelet or play with it as long as she is small, so that it won't be lost. And later on she cannot sell it. And be careful that it isn't stolen, for it is needed for the return voyage.'

Felicia's mother shrugged, and whenever afterward the bracelet was mentioned she always said 'that monster' or 'that horror.' Felicia's father had said, 'thank you, mother, that is a very precious gift for the little one' (he seldom said so much) and it sounded sad, especially that 'little one'—Felicia almost had to cry. But she did not, her grandmother certainly wouldn't approve—proud, be proud . . .

A while later they were rowed away in the proa and the old lady stood very upright under the trees and waved with a little batiste handkerchief; behind her stood the old servants, dressed in black, waving with their large starched handkerchiefs—the slave bell was rung incessantly—Felicia and her father waved and waved.

Felicia did not dare look left or right, it was almost as if her father were crying; her mother was staring straight ahead without waving—could she be crying too? But no, impossible!

'May I hold my box?' she asked.

'Yes,' said her father, who always said yes, and gave it to her, wiped his eyes and blew his nose.

Felicia sat there quite still with the box in her hand, she wasn't going to open it to look at her Snake with the Carbuncle stone; not now. 'Be careful that you don't drop that monster into the water,' said her mother.

Felicia looked at her without answering—her eyes *did* look red—'who were those three girls?' she asked.

'What girls?' said her mother.

'The girls grandma talked about that day she was angry with you, the girls who died.'

Her father was going to say something but her mother stopped him immediately. 'I don't want you to discuss that nonsense with the child,' she said, and to Felicia, 'oh nothing!—three girls who died long ago,' and she dismissed them with her hand.

After a time they rounded the cape to the outer bay and to the town, and later they went on from there to Europe.

THAT MORNING the boat from Java entered the outer bay ahead of schedule and slowly steamed up to the town. A light morning mist was hanging low over bay and town and mountains: as if the island were still tucked in and sleeping, without interest in the new morning or in a ship that happened to arrive or in anything.

On deck at the rail stood a young woman: small and strong with a round boyish face, springy brown hair, dark attentive eyes under frowning eyebrows. She wore clothes that didn't quite suit her: an elegant but faded dress, a little hat that had once been fashionable, thin stockings, shoes with worn high heels—Felicia who was coming back to the Small Garden at the inner bay where her grandmother would be waiting for her as she had once promised.

There were many people on the quay; she did not see her grandmother among them—perhaps she had died in the meantime, the voyage had taken months. Then what? What would she do then?

But as soon as the gangplank was out an old man and woman approached her—were they servants?—neatly dressed in black: the woman in black slippers with the toes pointing upward and with a starched and folded, snowy-white handkerchief in her hand. There were also two big children with them—children, grandchildren?—all four were dark, with curly hair, bareheaded and on bare feet except for the woman in her slippers.

She and her husband each took Felicia by one hand and told her their names and those of the children; Biblical first names, last names with many A's and U's, pointing to each other and talking and laughing, all very quickly and at the same time. The old woman sobbed just once and sniffed loudly without using the folded handkerchief.

Felicia did not recognize them, she did not remember the names, and couldn't understand the Malayan any more; she just nodded and laughed, she could have cried too—why not!

They came with her through the lounge to her cabin; there they bent over the basket, looked at each other. They clapped their hands, shook their heads, called—oh Lord, oh Lord!—as if they had never before seen a small child.

Felicia had bathed the little boy beforehand, fed him and dressed him neatly: a jacket of real Brussels lace (the last present from her mother) over his shirt and diaper. He had been sleeping quietly in his basket but now he woke up. He was a nice sturdy boy with some strands of dark hair, large light-brown eyes which he always opened very wide as if astonished at all he saw.

The old man immediately went to get coolies for the luggage; he urged them—come on, come on, we have to get going. They were in each other's way in the small cabin: Felicia had the child in her arms, the old man and the old woman carried the basket between them, the children took some bags and a rag doll over which they quarreled first, the coolies dragged the trunks out. Felicia had said goodbye to everyone the night before, she could get off now without delay.

At the end of the quay there was a carriage waiting with green wooden shutters, like a palanquin, with a coachman on the box, a team of small horses: it was the only coach on the island. All the bystanders gaped at them and the faces of the two children were radiant with pleasure at so much attention.

They went at a walk through the Chinese quarter with its little shops, and past a market. The old man kept sticking his head out of the window to make certain the coolies were following with the trunks, and every time the old woman held him tightly by his long coat so that he would not fall out of the decrepit coach—that made him angry and he tried to pull loose; the two children giggled.

There were not many people on the street yet, but those who were stopped to look and to salute.

A large square, lined with trees, a path along the walls, the walls of a fortress, to a small embankment under an awning.

The fog began to lift.

Everywhere there stood high trees in heavy foliage, right down to the edge of the outer bay; in the ditches and along the path, on the walls of the fortress too, grass grew and weeds and bushes—the whole world was very green that morning; and through the tightness of the tree trunks again and again the moving water of the bay with the silver reflections of the sun, the light traces on the blue of the surf from the sea; above it motionless the dark wavy coastline of the other shore, and above that a still-misty sky.

At the embankment a large winged proa was moored, and a smaller one for the luggage, with rowers and a helmsman.

The men climbed out of the proa and helped them

46

descend from the coach; the old man pointed to Felicia
and from her to the rowers. Felicia nodded, laughed; the
rowers nodded and laughed too, looked at the child on
her arm in its beautiful jacket, well, well!

When the coolies got there with the luggage it was immediately carried into the small proa; Felicia wanted to
get her purse but the old man produced an old-fashioned
lady's reticule of worn gray cloth, with a little silver lock,
and started to count out the money very solemnly: for the
coachman, for the coolies—one by one. Everyone interfered, they quarreled and came to agreements with a lot
of shouts and laughter.

Felicia stood there, watching, and all of a sudden she
recognized the purse: it was the household purse of her
grandmother—my purse, please bring me my purse, granddaughter—she was sure, and now she remembered: this
was the path behind the Castle, this was the quay from
which she left with Susanna and her father to go visit
the Small Garden at the inner bay. She had come back.

The old man and the two children climbed into the
bow of the big proa. Felicia sat on the middle bench with
the boy in her lap—he could already sit up straight, but
not for long. The old woman next to her held over their
heads a parasol of oiled paper, painted gaudily with flowers
and large butterflies; the child stared at it with wide-open
eyes. Their proa was pushed off and led the way; the
other one followed.

The rowers, two on each side, scooped up the water
with short broad oars; at first they had to push hard but
once the proa had gained speed they put in their oars
only occasionally. The helmsman aft steered with an

oar too, a few strokes on the left, then a few on the right; sometimes the proa rested with one wing on the water, sometimes with a sharp thud it shifted onto the other one.

The sun had burned away the mist, yet it did not become clear, and the light remained a silvery white—very glaring.

There was a rustling and swishing all around them: the bay, the oars in and out of the water, the waves spattering against the boards of the proa and the beams of the wings; and when they rowed close to the shore the mild surf on the sand and against the coral reefs; the wind in the trees. And beneath these sounds the old woman talked and talked in a monotonously muttering voice—when she remembered that Felicia did not understand she stopped and smiled shyly behind the pleated white handkerchief.

After a while the boy became sleepy and Felicia put him in the basket which was standing at her feet. The old woman immediately held the parasol over the basket and no longer over their heads; she said something again, pointed with a finger at Felicia, 'ex-act grand-ma,' she said laboriously, and pointing at the boy who was dozing contentedly in the light and the rustle and the small movement of the proa, 'ex-act mas-ter Wil-lem' and she made a gesture in the direction they were going.

Did she want to say that her grandmother had thus come back with her little son Willem to the Small Garden at the inner bay, once?

Perhaps this same woman had been there—Felicia's father would be fifty soon, had he been a few years old then? Between forty-five and fifty years ago?

The old woman would have been barely twenty. Now

48

in her late sixties, as old as the grandmother—Felicia was
calculating it all very carefully as if it were terribly important: more than forty-five, almost fifty years ago—that
is not so very long ago, it might have been today.

She was sitting there with head bent forward to get
some shade from the parasol, she stared at the boy—her
grandmother with her little son Willem in the proa, with
a nurse? or perhaps a native playmate from the Garden
who had come along when she married her 'beau' and
went with him to Java—far away, and now she was coming back—what kind of man would that husband of her
grandmother have been, who had died so young?

She had never thought about that before—she was
constantly thinking now of things she had never thought
about before: in the light and the rustle and the small
movement of the proa.

Her own husband had been a 'foreigner' in a hotel in
Nice: no wonder, she and her parents had always lived
in hotels in Europe—'not another day,' her mother would
cry, and off to the next hotel. A handsome, distinguished
foreigner, 'he looks like a diplomat,' said her mother, who
had been enchanted with him—Felicia too had been
enchanted with him but hadn't said it; her father had
said nothing at all, as usual. And he?—'that sugary money
of your mother's,' he sometimes said when they were
alone together. He had a lightly mocking way of speaking,
sometimes a bit melancholy too.

With the 'sugary money' everything had had to be
paid—he had been involved in an 'affair of honor' in his
own country and could not return there. No one understood exactly what he had lived on until then.

They had been married, traveled a lot, lived in hotels too, expensive hotels, sometimes with the parents, sometimes alone; they had used up quite a bit of the 'sugary money.' Her mother had approved, she took care of all their affairs—five years; then came the sugar crisis in Java.

Felicia was finally expecting the child which she had expected all those years—in a room in an expensive hotel and without money; there was nothing the man knew how to do, she could play the piano—a note stuck in the frame of the mirror: to America, and try—a new life for her and the child, and later—he had been obliged to take some of her jewels for the voyage, just for the time being, there was no other way—and—Li—that was how he called her.

He had taken with him all that was left of the 'sugary money,' and all her jewels and the Snake with the Carbuncle stone—he should not have done that, she had told him about the Snake with the Carbuncle stone. He also should not have gone before the child was there, before he had seen the child . . .

When the child was a few months old she had borrowed money from relatives in Holland for the voyage back; her father had for once in his life said, 'that is good, we belong at the Small Garden'; her mother had been angry, 'now you're taking little Willem away from us too, now I'll never go walking with him or buy him something,' and she had cried. In the end she had somehow found the money for that jacket which was much too expensive.

Her grandmother, newly widowed, was returning home

in the proa with her son Willem—yes, that's the way things sometimes work out, granddaughter.

The child in the basket was called Willem after his grandfather and she was alone too. They were going back to have a roof over their heads and a bite to eat; and she must try and raise her little son—oh, he'd grow up, she thought, and he'd have a wife and child later; who knows, a daughter? the daughter would marry one day and her son would be called Willem after his own grandfather Willem; the daughter's husband would die or go away— to America for instance, that is far away, and then she would—'that's the way things work out, granddaughter, yes!' Who? who was saying that? was she, Felicia, saying that to her granddaughter?—no, that did not make sense, that wasn't it—she herself was the granddaughter—

She thought, she had never before thought that—in the light and the rustle and the small movement of the proa—repetition, repetition, nothing but repetitions linked to one another. Again and again the same, and again and once more.

The old man in the bow called out, she did not hear him; the old woman touched her. He was pointing: to the right a low cape which seemed to block off the outer bay, to the left the inner bay, enclosed in green shores like a lake—somewhere there was the Garden. She nodded— yes, yes, for sure—who cares.

The proa no longer followed the coast but set out to cross the inner bay—was there nothing within reach to break into pieces, nothing she could smash?

She bent over the edge of the proa, scooped up water

in her hand—the water was cool—she dabbed her face with it, pulled off that silly hat, another splash of water—her hair wet too!—sat up straight: she wasn't her grandmother, and not her granddaughter either! She, who was named Felicia—Happy—that was her name, she came with her child for a stay with its great-grandmother (how many children have a great-grandmother?) in the Garden at the bay—where was there a more beautiful bay?

The child would play there as she had, with shell and coral, with duck crabs on little red legs, with tame birds; he would be afraid of the Leviathan and the palm-wine mannikin; a child must have something to be afraid of too. The fishermen would take him in their proas and teach him to call out—Mister Wind—and would a child not be happy then?

And she was no 'widow woman'—her husband was still alive, whatever had happened, he was still alive. For a moment she put her cool wet hand together with the warm dry one in her lap—let him stay alive, she asked, amen . . .

She unclasped her hands again, nudged the old woman, pointed at the boy in the basket, 'not Willem!' she said, 'not Willem,' moving her lips spasmodically and all the while shaking her head. What was his name then? She couldn't think of a name so quickly, 'not Willem! Willy! Willy!'

The face of the old woman, first tense in her effort to understand, relaxed, she nodded, she understood very well—not mas-ter Willem, but Himpies! Immediately she called through the proa to the others—Himpies!—and pointed, and then they began: helmsman and rowers, the old man and woman, the two big children, they began to sing the song of the boy Himpies of the island Saparua who had a tummy of rubber.

One whistled his part, another improvised a deep bass, the old man suddenly had a piece of wood in his hand and beat out the rhythm on the edge of the proa, the two children clapped their hands, the old woman pushed the folded handkerchief into her sleeve, gave Felicia the parasol—quickly, she wanted to clap her hands too.

Felicia held the parasol and tried to listen to what they sang, she didn't understand much of it, only the chorus—Himpies, little boy Himpies, of the island Saparua.

The boy Himpies in the basket woke up; first he turned over on his stomach, on knees and elbows, then with a jolt and a turn he sat up straight in his crumpled lace jacket and looked dumfounded over the basket's edge; he was soaking wet.

Thus they arrived at the Small Garden on the inner bay.

The slave bell was being rung.

The grandmother was standing under the trees on the beach in an orange silk sarong and white jacket, high-heeled slippers, with a little kerchief in her hand as if she had been standing there through all those seventeen years. She was a bit smaller and darker, but her hair had not yet turned gray.

'There you are, granddaughter,' she said, 'I have been waiting for you, and did you bring your little boy Willem?'

'His name is Himpies, grandma.'

'Do you think that's such a beautiful name? All right! Good day, Himpies,' said the old lady, 'welcome,' and she tried to shake hands with him as if he were a grown man, 'I have already started a cabinet with curiosities for you.'

Then she led them in, up the stone stairway to the wide side gallery and to their room. It was the front one, the prettiest of all four, and it had once been the room of Felicia's parents. Their English brass bed was still standing there with all the knobs Felicia had always wanted to count as a child; and her own crib with its wooden bars on each side.

A tall thin woman was moving about the room, not as neatly dressed in black as the others, in a colored sarong and long jacket, a bit rumpled.

'This is Sjeba, granddaughter,' said the grandmother, 'and this is my granddaughter, Sjeba, who has come back with her little son Willem, I mean Himpies. Don't you remember each other?'

'No,' said Sjeba, 'we don't remember each other,' she spoke some words of broken Dutch; she took the little boy from Felicia, 'you come here little boy Himpies, and I'll change you.'

The child looked at her, opened his eyes even wider than usual, pulled his chin in; and then he laughed for the first time at his other mother Sjeba.

Felicia walked farther into the room: from the windows there was the view through the trees on the inner bay;

for the rest there were only doors, a large double door to the side gallery, a door to her grandmother's bedroom, and yet another door leading to stone steps which went down to the garden, near the lemon orchard.

It was a large room and it contained the usual furniture: some dressers, a rattan towel rack, a wash stand with a marble top and a flowery basin, a Japanese screen around a night commode, a coat stand with white curtains, chairs and a table. On the marble tabletop stood a little bunch of flowers, a glass with oil and a wick for a night light. On the walls hung heavily decorated oil lamps.

'Where have the three girls gone to?' Felicia asked.

The grandmother looked at her. 'The three girls? How do you mean?'

'Who were on the screen of the night lamp.'

'Oh those, you mean those! You still remember, grand-daughter,' she would often say these words that day, 'of course they are still here, wait!' She walked out of the room and came back with a little glass screen which she put on the table, 'these girls?'

It was a screen of pink milky glass in a frame of black wrought iron on curved legs: under a pink tree two pink girls were sitting on a seesaw and a third pink girl was watching them, with a hoop and a stick in her hand—all three in the same stiff pink dresses with flounces, high-buttoned shoes, pink picture hats with ribbons; a little pink dog was jumping around, in the pink sky a swarm of pink swallows—far off—were on their way to the pink south.

'Yes, those girls!' Felicia said; now the screen was where it had always been and at night the light would shine through it again, a pink night light.

'Think of you remembering that, granddaughter!'

In the grandmother's room not much had been changed; Felicia looked for a moment at the cabinet on the legs with the claws—but on that first day she did not ask anything about the 'special drawer,' the treasure, the guardians of good fortune; the grandmother did not speak about it either. It still smelled of incense in the room, the real Arabian, the tears of the prophet.

Next to it the guest room, of course there had to be a guest room.

And the last room, farthest in back, was sitting room and dining room both: the old black piano, a round dining table in the middle under a hanging oil lamp with the antique chairs around it, a little buffet, a cupboard, in one of the corners a rattan chair. On the walls blue china plates were hung in a neat row—everything exactly as it used to be.

But there was a little red lacquered cabinet which Felicia did not recall: in the bottom were drawers, above them two glass doors. The grandmother immediately took her there, 'the curiosities cabinet for Himpies!' she said.

Behind the glass doors things were still standing without order: on the top shelves china and glassware for parties, green wine glasses, a large teacup, white with gold—On Your Anniversary—a silver ice bucket (as if there were ever ice on the island), mother-of-pearl spoons.

On the shelf below stood a basket filled with fruits cut from the softest inner core of the sago palm and painted in bright colors—behind it a stuffed bird of paradise was perched on a little branch: its tail upright like a fountain of yellow and gold, its green satin head bent as if it were picking a fruit.

On the next shelf, coral: at the back and on the sides transparent 'sea fans,' and in the center the finest of all, the 'sea net' and the 'sea linen' in quenched purple and dark yellow; a piece of 'sea string,' and a little tree of black coral. A large shell, a 'Triton's horn,' was there too, orange red inside, with a nice round hole 'for Himpies to blow on.'

The grandmother also opened the top drawer, full of little shells, one had been set aside from the others, and she said, 'that is the double Venus-heart, granddaughter, that is a very rare one.'

The books of Mr. Rumphius had been put in the bottom drawer.

In the side gallery there were potted plants between the pillars; and there was a couch with a flowery spread and a low round table in front of it.

And just as in the past some tame birds were walking through the house, two green parakeets together and a little black parrot with a lame leg; they could go about freely, there were never any cats or dogs in the Small Garden.

The little boy had to be taken care of, his porridge cooked and fed to him, and then he went to sleep again in his basket. Felicia and her grandmother ate together, rested a bit, unpacked; Sjeba helped with everything.

And every now and again Felicia stepped out into the garden: to the right, the foundations of the old spicegrower's house were still visible among the nutmeg trees, and farther down that way was the green valley with all the fowl, the wild little river, and the one large white shell of the Leviathan—oh, it was just the drinking place for the chickens.

Behind the house the wood—the three neglected graves; she did not continue into the hills but walked the other way down to the wide river under the trees, with the village on the other shore.

It was all different from the way she had thought it to be.

In the house, the old pavilion, she had found the furniture, the things of the past—old and worn, true, but they were still there; and people went about, her grandmother, servants, their children, and a few birds.

The house, the outbuildings especially with their thick walls, were standing solidly enough; the bronze slave bell was still hanging in its wooden bell tower.

Out in the open: the hills with the rosebushes, the dark rocks toward the valley; the trees and the palms in the wood and everywhere—one even more graceful, tall or leafy than the other—the planes on the small strip of beach, so regal in faded silvery gray and darkest green; the living water everywhere—the Small Garden! And yet, how could there be any place in the world so deserted and still and abandoned? A bit sad, a bit sallow in color, 'poorish,' as her mother always said, in the merciless white sunlight—and so terribly and hopelessly far away from everything and from everyone.

The large kitchen in one of the outbuildings was full of people talking and laughing, but it was as if their voices came from somewhere else.

The grandmother went to look there from time to time

and asked her to come along. She saw new faces each time, heard new names—they had endlessly long names.

'Who are they all?' she asked, 'do you have so many servants?'

'But of course not, granddaughter,' said her grandmother, 'how can you think that? Only those two who came to the boat to get you, the old Eliah and Sarah, those are my own servants from long ago—Sarah and I have known each other all our lives; Sarah is my friend. Their son Henry is now the cowherd and Sjeba is his wife—you know her too now—they have no children; another son, Moses, is the gardener; the two children who came to the boat with them are from still another son. They go to the school in town, they are so bright, Josua and Susanna. Today they were excused to go to the boat.'

'My nanny once was also called Susanna.'

'Yes, the fat one,' grandmother said—but she did not go on about 'once.'

'And all those others?' asked Felicia.

'They work in the garden occasionally, or row me. Some of them have come only to see Himpies. When he wakes up, you must take him over so that they can see him.'

Later the boy was put on a mat under a tree and people came to look at him in little groups, never too many at a time; they talked to him, sang him a song. The boy watched them silently and solemnly, with the rag doll under his arm; the two big children Josua and Susanna were sitting next to him and Sjeba did not let him out of her sight.

Felicia finished unpacking, put things away in the dressers; her grandmother helped her, she enjoyed it, looked at everything, chatted, asked questions. Her husband's name was not mentioned between them on that day, nor ever afterward; she also said little about 'your mother,' but she often mentioned 'my son Willem, my son Willem.' When they had finished she asked, 'you have none of your jewels left, granddaughter, how did that happen? your mother bought—there were so many jewels—did you have to sell everything after the sugar crisis? What a pity! but you had your bracelet for the voyage, was it enough for the voyage?'

Felicia said that it had not been enough for the voyage; she had had to borrow money from a relative of her mother's, the same one who was for the time being supporting her parents.

'Oh!' said the grandmother, startled, 'but then you have a debt, granddaughter—a debt must be paid.'

Evening fell early and the first day had passed.

Felicia had put the child with basket and all in the big double bed under the mosquito curtain—he couldn't fall out that way; that first night she did not want him to sleep in a strange crib.

The night lamp shone through the pink screen and in the side gallery a large oil lamp was burning.

'Why don't you leave the door to the gallery open?' the grandmother said. 'It is nice and cool, and they can have their look at Himpies; they won't wake him.'

For in the dark people were still crossing the river and walking with torches toward the house and the large lit-up kitchen. And Felicia saw men and women, sometimes a man or a woman alone, old or young, go to her room; the men stayed at the door, the women went in—not for long, who would want to look for long at a sleeping child!—and Sjeba would be around somewhere to watch. She and her grandmother were sitting on the strip of beach together in the cool evening breeze, right in front of the house—the lamplight from the side gallery shone through the trees.

It was high tide; the little waves came almost up to their feet.

'There are all sorts of treats for them,' the grandmother said, 'turtle meat with herbs—it has been cooking all day in a thick bamboo, which gives it a special flavor of its own, and Sarah is very good at frying fish with kanari nuts and peppers, she must show you too, granddaughter; and there are sago breads, black and white mussel sauces, both of them. There is fresh palm wine which won't get them drunk very quickly and—' she winked—'a bit of good arak which I still had, and coffee of course.'

'For all these people! But doesn't that cost too much money?' Felicia asked worriedly.

'It must be,' said her grandmother, 'that's the way it is done; it is because they have come for Himpies, and it is all from the Garden—except the arak, which I had saved; it usually serves as a medicine, you know.'

Felicia had moved her chair so that she could see past the open door of the room where the child was sleeping and through the side gallery to the outbuildings. In the kitchen was singing; someone played on a kind of guitar, another blew on a bamboo flute with little runs and trills.

Where they were sitting there was the sound of the water.

'Are you listening to the bay? You are so silent, grand-daughter—three waves behind each other—the father, the mother, the child, they say here, can you hear it?' and the old woman repeated it once more with the waves.

Felicia came back from far off: here she was, sitting as she had wanted to, on the beach of the Garden on the island in the Moluccas, listening to the surf—the father, the mother, the child—better not say it! just say the child . . . the child . . . and obediently the waves went on in a whisper the child . . . the child . . . the child.

'Do you still have cows, grandma?'

'Yes, granddaughter.'

'And chickens and ducks too, I saw.'

'Yes, for the eggs.'

'And do you still have a vegetable garden and all those fruit trees?'

'Yes, certainly, granddaughter'—the old woman hesitated for a moment, what were these questions leading up to?—'The red grapefruit, do you remember that one?'

Felicia looked her way in the half-dark. 'Why don't we try to sell all those things in the town at the outer bay— milk, eggs, vegetables, fruits? And you used to make pickles and candied fruits and mussel sauce, and also scents and amber balls and bracelets against rheumatism—can you teach me too, grandma?'

The grandmother moved a bit forward in her chair and sat up straight as if she had swallowed a broom, 'what do you mean, granddaughter? sell? for money? we! you can't mean that, we didn't pay money for those things. Our animals give milk and eggs, fruits are from the garden, mussels from the bay—black coral the fishermen bring me because I give them medicine when they are ill—the only thing is sugar, cane sugar for candied fruits, you can't use palm sugar for that. I used to get it every year from your mother's plantation, from Java—a large round hamper of white sugar—I don't any longer. And for amber balls I have to buy everything, and gold of course, that's not from the Garden.

'But it isn't necessary to make candied fruits! And as a matter of fact I still have a lot of jars of them, and amber balls in gold are not necessary either, I haven't made those in years and years—but I remember the recipes for the amber and the candied fruits quite well . . . ' She fell silent, out of breath almost.

Felicia pretended not to have heard the end of it, 'well, you see that you have to buy things too, and you have to pay people for their work, and work yourself . . . ' She put out her hand and took the hand of the old woman with the black coral branch around the thin wrist, 'the work of your hands,' she said.

'Yes, granddaughter, but our hands we have received too—free as a gift for nothing to keep—' (as she used to say). She did not pull her hand back and after a time only said, 'I understand, you mean to say that we have to earn money: your debt!' she whispered, and aloud again, 'and for Himpies, who must go to school, yes, that is good—he has to learn a great deal and become clever. Would he want to become a doctor, do you think? Then he can have my snakestone, remember? So we'll become two trades-women together'—she grinned—'a tradeswoman can be proud too, can't she, granddaughter?'

They had got up and gone into the house, the grandmother had shown her how to close the doors and the blinds, open the slats, 'you don't have to be afraid,' she had said, 'it is safe here.' Was she thinking of the sentinels in the 'special drawer'?

She had helped Felicia lift the basket off the bed and had remained to watch her change the little boy, who slept through it all, put a rubber mat in the bed on the wall side and lay the child on top of that. She had kissed Felicia good night, 'you undress, and I'll come back later to tuck in the mosquito curtain,' she had promised.

'Sleep well, granddaughter, in the Small Garden, together with Himpies.' Felicia was tired, but she lay awake a long time. It wasn't dark, the night lamp shone pink through the screen with the three girls—after so many nights aboard the ship, in a little cabin on a narrow bunk, the bed seemed so large and wide; and the child lay next to her, small and lost in that vague space, between wide plains of sheet and mosquito net—it wasn't quite still outside: the light surf of the inner bay, sometimes the sighing of the wind in the trees close to the house, the voices from the outbuilding as from very far—would they dance on the spice platform? sing? the bamboo flute sounded clearly, meltingly sweet, from very close—

'The double Venus-heart—that is a very rare one, granddaughter.'

Tomorrow she would ask her grandmother if there wasn't a single bed to be found somewhere, at the house in the town perhaps.

AFTER ONLY a few days the grandmother sent Felicia with the child and Sjeba to the town at the outer bay to pay visits, 'that is the proper way—who arrives must greet,' she said.

She had prepared a list of names beforehand, and told her who all the people were and why they had to be called on: only from politeness or because they could advise her, perhaps later be of help. She should first just leave her name, and pay all calls in the sequence of the list—and stay here so long and there so long. She also gave Felicia little presents to take with her, jars with preserves, mussel sauces (black and white), lemonades—for them, and for them!

Then she should pay a morning call on the wife of the 'Captain of the Chinese' and some other Chinese ladies in the quarter; and the 'Lieutenant of the Arabs'—he was an influential man and very jealous of the 'Captain' although he didn't show it. On no account could she go on these visits alone: she should take Himpies and Sjeba, and also the two big children Josua and Susanna, 'first ask the school to give them the morning off,' and the caretaker and his wife and children who lived in the town house when there was no one there.

'Be careful, they should all be dressed neatly.' And the more people she showed up with, the more elegant—pity that the palanquin was so expensive. She didn't have to say much on those visits; just laugh in a friendly way every

now and then, 'and remember, don't get up to leave too
quickly, that isn't proper.'

She should try to make friends with the owners of the
two hotels—one was a lady, the other a gentleman—hotels
always needed all sorts of things—and also on her
evening visit with the military doctor, if she dared—he was
the head of the little military hospital, in a hospital they
needed things too.

She would stay in the town house and Sjeba would
take care of everything.

When she returned the grandmother immediately
wanted to know everything: how they had received her in
the town at the outer bay, and what he had said, and she,
and whether they had been friendly to Himpies, and to
her.

Felicia related: everyone in the town had been friendly
to Himpies, and to her; and he had said this and she had
said that—and if she wanted she could also give piano
lessons in the town, there was no one there who did.

'Do you now want to give piano lessons, granddaughter,
and for money too!'

And when Felicia asked why they didn't redecorate the
house in the town and rent it, the old lady was even more
indignant than before, 'what do you mean, rent our house?
for money? we? you don't mean it,' but after a while
she gave in again, 'all right then, for Himpies, and that—';
the other 'that' she didn't mention aloud, and she sighed.

The town at the outer bay was deeply moved: the poor
'young lady of the Small Garden' (that's what they
called her), not even twenty-five years old and left with
a child to take care of all alone, a husband who had walked

out on her, or she on him? and then to come here, to
an old grandmother on an old neglected spice garden,
and with the prices which spices fetched nowadays, they
would have to content themselves with a dish of sago
porridge and a fish from the bay. And then, to start a
little trade, and not even be ashamed to talk about it! It
would never work of course: you had to be born to a
thing like that.

But after a few years the town on the outer bay had
changed its tune. In that time Felicia and her grandmother
had made the Small Garden into a kind of model farm:
milk, fresh chicken eggs and salted duck eggs, vegetables,
fruits, mushrooms could all be bought there; and pickles,
preserves and mussel sauces, but those had to be ordered
in advance.

Early in the morning the milk proa moored under the
awning behind the Castle: the bottles with milk and the
baskets of vegetables were picked up, the empties returned; one of the servants managed everything. Felicia
often came along, she taught piano in town, and she went
to the Chinese quarter—never alone, grandmother still
did not allow that—to negotiate with a Chinese or Arab
merchant about 'the other things' these merchants bought
and resold, the things one was not supposed to talk about,
no one in town was to know of—everyone knew!—medicinal herbs, dried scents, mixed incense, but especially
black coral bracelets against rheumatism, with or without gold decoration, and amber balls in golden-fretted
fruits.

Those 'other things' eventually went everywhere, to the
other islands and even farther, to Java and Sumatra and

all the way to Malacca: most of the money was earned with them.

In the beginning it was earned by the merchant only; but then one morning the grandmother sent the gala proa and invited him for a visit with her at the Garden—there she had him sit on the couch in the side gallery and have a glass of homemade vanilla lemonade with kanari cake, and the old grandmother sat next to him and looked at him a few times—and from then on things worked out quite satisfactorily.

They had been lucky—not too unlucky—with the Small Garden. What was planted grew; the animals were healthy, the people content. The goldsmith from the town came to live there—there was so much work for him, and every few months the old woman came, the bibi, from whom the grandmother bought everything which was not 'from here'; also the ambergris, also the gold. Ambergris and gold were weighed against each other and were equally expensive. No one else was allowed to attend those negotiations, not even Felicia at first.

The family house in the town had been rented well: one pavilion room was kept for Felicia to sleep in when she stayed in town. The spices fetched reasonable prices.

The sugar crisis passed; Felicia's parents could subsist again, although her mother never stopped complaining. She had immediately hired 'legal counsel' (as she called it) to trace Felicia's husband in America. In North America? In South America? Don't you know even that much? She assumed he had married again—then we can have him prosecuted for bigamy, they are very severe with that in America, and he'll end in prison where he be-

longs! And then Felicia would be able to get a divorce and
'start a new life,' she wrote; otherwise she would have to
wait at least five years—she was angry when Felicia didn't
answer her on this. And then she offered to pay the
debt, fussed for years about the exact amount—and didn't
she need a new piano in that wilderness? She sent parcels
with beautiful clothes for the little boy, who never wore
them.

Felicia's father, as always, wrote a monthly note to his
mother and added—many warm greetings to Felicia and
the little Willem.

The boy Himpies grew up, a pretty child, a sweet child
too, healthy, content, everyone liked him. Yet he was
not spoiled: he could never be found, they always had to
search for him—for him and his slightly older friend,
Domingoes, the son of the goldsmith and his young wife
who had lived for such a long time at the Small Garden.

It seemed as if the Garden took the two children away
and hid them: in all the water, the cistern, the rivers,
the shallow inner bay; in all the green, the trees, the wood,
the rosebushes on the hills and the forests behind the hills
at the foot of the mountains—once they lost their way
there and were found in the dead of night only, by a
torchlight party.

They secretly crossed the river to the village and hid in
the hut of the man with the blue hair to listen to the
stories about his son. The fishers took them along in their
proas, or they played underneath a proa on the beach—
who was going to keep track of the two children?

The grandmother was ailing at times but always recovered and immediately went back to work—the endless jobs

of patience: the trimming of the black coral, softening it in oil, warming it, bending it very carefully, and again, and again, until a bracelet was in its proper shape and could set; and after a while the goldsmith decorated it with gold motifs or with gold snake heads and tails.

The weighing, the painstaking powdering of ambergris and black amber, with benzoin and musk and rose water and ground rasamala roots added for body, to make the amber balls. The goldsmith did the fretwork on the golden fruits which held the balls.

The mussel sauces took more time than anything: the rinsing of the mussels—not a single grain of sand should be left in them, her honor was at stake there.

She was always curious to see how a thing would turn out, and that made the monotonous work yet a bit adventurous.

And thus life at the Small Garden unrolled its peaceful course.

But Felicia was not peaceful: things were always tugging at her. On one side the town at the outer bay, not even so very far from the Garden but turned away from it, as if belonging to another world—over there . . .

The town of possibilities: ships which came and went once a month—with a ship someone might arrive, someone else might leave . . .

A post office with mail coming in and going out—a letter can be sent in the mail, from one side or from the other, but there has to be an address on the envelope—

The town also of the evening parties: in the beginning Felicia was asked to all the parties, for there was always a shortage of young European women and girls, everyone was prepared to close an eye as far as her 'trade' was concerned. Dressed up in an evening gown from the past, with the real tortoise-and-gold fan from her grandmother's youth on a ribbon around her wrist, she danced through the long warm tropical night, danced, danced, with him and with him, she loved dancing—you dance well, Li—nobody called her Li. Afterward some polite young man took her home, to the pavilion room of the town house, along one of the paths lined with high trees, in the moonlight, in the night.

In the town at the outer bay it was stated that there wasn't much fun in seeing the young lady of the Small Garden home at night in the moonlight.

And on the other side, the Garden which pulled her back across the outer bay to the blue movement of the inner bay, to its own deep green silence—where the two children, Himpies and Domingoes, were standing at the quay, hand in hand, waiting for her; a little farther down the old grandmother was waiting, and the faithful Sjeba, always—to all the jobs she liked to do, to all the money she earned with her work, and the feeling of security it gave her.

In the end the Garden won. Her clothes helped in its victory. When the French dresses, shoes and stockings were worn out, she first tried: a pattern from the magazine *Gracieuse*, drawing paper, a piece of material from the Chinese quarter, her grandmother and Sjeba fitted her—it didn't look like much, she thought, and she began turning down the invitations to the evening parties in town. After that she dressed for a while in white cottons which didn't become her at all, and walked on high-heeled slippers which made her teeter; then in sarong and jacket. Not bright silk sarongs like her grandmother: a strong yellow and brown batik sarong from Java, a white jacket without any frills, and her bare feet in low-heeled leather sandals. She canceled the piano lessons, made the merchants come to see her when that was necessary, and only rarely went to the town at the outer bay.

The Garden held her, slowly enveloped her, showed her things, whispered her its secrets . . .

And Sjeba showed her the way through the forest on the high mountains beyond the hills to the little spring: she scooped up the crystal water with her hand and drank it—bitter, bitter! Sjeba had warned her—she could say a thing like that so vehemently, and also that once you had taken that water in your mouth you should never spit it out again . . .

Felicia read what Mr. Rumphius had said about the coral woman and she visited the place where the coral woman had drowned and been fished up again later.

Now she also heard the story of the three little girls.

After a long day Felicia and her grandmother caught their breath before going to bed, sitting in chairs at the beach or in the gallery on the couch, or just on a mat with their feet dangling over the garden; not speaking much, the grandmother repeating some advice or a recipe, 'so that you won't forget.'

That evening rain had threatened but it had stayed dry—very hot, very dark—a gleam of light from the side gallery fell on the open space in front of them where the stone foundations of the old house were standing, the one Felicia's mother had wanted to rebuild, which had started the quarrel and had made them go to Europe, had made her meet a stranger in a hotel in Nice, had made her—made her—the nutmeg trees grew close around it . . .

The old woman leaned against the stone pillar, she had been ill, 'granddaughter, I have to tell you something,' and she fell silent.

'Tell me, grandma.'

'The house must not be rebuilt!' said the grandmother.

'Oh, that, I know that, you didn't want it that time and now—don't think we're going to spend our good money on a thing like that.'

'It is not a matter of money,' the old woman said impatiently, 'you will have plenty of money some day, and it isn't that I am afraid either—' she waited a moment —'my father,' she then said, 'my father was the younger brother of the three girls, much younger! He never even saw them.'

'You've never told me that, grandma.'

'Oh,' she said.

And then she told the story of the first spicegrower, a large family with many children, who had lived in the beautiful house, 'the spices fetched so much money!' with the white marble hall on the second floor ('the spice ships brought the marble from Europe, as ballast'), with the many slaves.

There had been a slave market on the island of Ternate where they went to buy them—Papua slaves were rather cheap—slaves from Bali for instance were very expensive.

The nurse of the three eldest daughters had been a slave girl from Bali, 'she was so beautiful, granddaughter, everyone thought her so beautiful—including, I think, the father of my father, the father of the three girls; and that's why the mother of the girls hated her and that's why she hated the mother of the girls—the one the other —yes, that is the way things can be!'

And she told how the three little girls had died—all three on one day, by poison? venom? 'you know—venom!' or from a disease? Nobody had ever known.

But once when the father was away from the island, the mother went to the police in the town at the outer bay and put in an accusation against the slave girl, and they had come for her and interrogated her in the Castle —they had examined her twice—'people were still put to torture then, granddaughter, and think, a slave!' She never confessed anything, not the second time either, but she was from Bali—the Balinese are very wise, they have means against pain—perhaps she knew means against pain; after that they had to let her go.

'My father said once—everyone had slaves, those were the years of the slaves, that was the evil of the time, my father said. Every time has its own evil, but a human being can still be good. In the years of the slaves a man could be good to his slaves, my father said—his father had been good, but his mother had not, his mother had been cruel. He said that of his own mother, granddaughter, and also that it wasn't true about the three girls, that his mother had only made that up—oh, nobody knows what happened, whose fault it was.

'The people here at the Garden have been saying through all these years, whenever they talk about their deaths, that the girls were poisoned, but they weren't there, they cannot know; my father said they hadn't been poisoned but he was not there either, he couldn't have known—nobody knows—oh, they should have had the poison plate from Ceram.

'The slave girl lived on for a long time, my father remembered her quite well—she had never been able to walk after it, he said, oh, granddaughter! Then she must have died, and the house came down in the bad earthquake and when it happened the mother of my father was up in the Hall with a little child (she had so many children) and they were buried under the stones and burned to death.

'My father said, "The house is a house of ill fortune, it must not be rebuilt, but don't think about the rest any more, don't talk about it! So that it will not happen all over again"; and now I have done it anyway, but who else—please repeat once so that you won't forget, just this: the house must not be rebuilt—you know now why not,' she whispered, 'you don't have to repeat that part of it.'

After Felicia had repeated it, the old woman sighed deeply and leaned against the pillar.

Felicia's voice had sounded gruff and reluctant, and that was how she felt: a deep unwillingness, an aversion —it required an effort to stay where she was—the child, Himpies, she should never have brought him here, to the Garden so far away, so far from God and all men, and hemmed in on all sides: rivers, inner bay, mountains, and on an island—hemmed in again—the sea around it, nowhere a little path leading to escape. A trap within a trap, and within, like those two women who had once hated each other—together in a trap—and the three small children! Now, it was different now, of course she realized that, and yet: Himpies in his little bed like—'grandma!' she called out aloud, 'was that house, is . . . is it, is the Small Garden—is there a curse on the Small Garden? Please tell me the truth.'

'A curse? You mustn't say such a thing, granddaughter. A house of ill luck, yes! But ill luck is not the same as a curse, and the Garden—the Small Garden? would it be —no, you don't think that, you can't think that. Wherever there are people there is also ill luck, sadness, evil too sometimes, venom, you know—venom—but that doesn't mean that we, that people are cursed, you mustn't say that, granddaughter. It is not good to say that.' The old woman was sitting up straight and she kept shaking her head; it took her a while to calm down. 'I know what you mean: when we meet evil it scares us, it frightens us, but it shouldn't. We must try to remain proud people, upright!'

She leaned back against the pillar and after a long time she said, 'when you want to preserve pineapple it is a good thing to soak it first overnight in lime water, grand-daughter.'

Felicia did not answer, she looked at her, 'sometimes you see things, don't you, grandma?' she asked.

'Yes,' the old woman answered hesitantly, 'sometimes it seems . . . but . . . but not very clearly.'

'Did you ever see the three girls?'

'I? I thought so, once, but it wasn't true.'

'And all the others here say—'

'You mustn't believe them!' said the old woman vehemently, 'they repeat each other, people always repeat each other—once, I hadn't been back for long at the Small Garden with my son Willem, and I was standing there—' she pointed behind the house where the wood began—'together with an old cook we had then; she died long since, you've never known her. She could see things. I was sad that day, I had spells of sadness in those days, like you now, don't you, granddaughter, and then suddenly she said, probably to console me, "look, mistress! the three girls, there they go, sssh," and when I asked, "but where?" she said, "there!" and she pointed under the trees, "don't you see them? there, all three, but hush," and she indicated with her hand how tall each one was: thus, and thus, and thus, and it was as if she really saw them. "They're sweet children," she said, "the two oldest like to laugh but the youngest one doesn't!" '

When Felicia went to bed, the room with its whitewashed walls, light-gray doors and blinds, with all the white gauze mosquito netting and draperies, was very still but so open and light in the pink radiation from the night lamp, so without any hint of nightly dark and fear and secrets—the child Himpies was sleeping in the crib: arms and legs spread wide he slept, withdrawn from everything—she stood and watched him for a moment. In future she would make him say good night to the three girls on the screen around the night lamp. Later he would hear about three other girls who had been made to drink poison, she could not prevent that; but he might confuse them all and think that Elsbet, Katie and Marregie were those three happy girls in pink: the two eldest on the seesaw and the smallest who did not laugh, with the hoop and stick. He wouldn't know who was who.

On top of all the other work Felicia now had the servants dig out the foundations of the old house: the debris, which was full of pieces of white marble, could well be used to reinforce the embankment at the inner bay.

Whatever she tried to plant on that spot afterward languished, and when she complained about it the grandmother looked at her, said nothing—only muttered something about foolishness!—what had she expected?

And the bibi . . .

At that same time, after her illness, the grandmother began to call Felicia in on her negotiations with the bibi, 'so you'll know how it's done.'

The bibi always stepped out of her proa by herself, and the bell was not rung either; the grandmother remained standing at the top of the stairs in the side gallery. But she did shake hands with the bibi and bade her sit down on the couch.

The bibi was small and thin, very dark; she wore an old sarong of many colors and a solid-colored jacket, very dark green or dark red but not black; a woven scarf over her head which she never took off. The servants who were Christians (on the Small Garden all servants were Christians and the village across the river was Christian too) whispered that she was a Mohammedan, that she had certainly been to Mecca and that Allah's name must be embroidered in that scarf—but who was going to ask her? As long as the bibi was there everyone kept at a distance.

The grandmother brought a tray from the living room with a plate and a cup and saucer which were used by the bibi only; they always stood apart from the other china. The bibi could not eat from a plate or drink from a cup which had been used by someone else. They also made separate coffee for her and a new jar of candied fruit was opened—the bibi had a sweet tooth. When Felicia once said, 'what a lot of bother!' the grandmother replied that that was the proper way to do it.

In the meantime the bibi unpacked her basket and put all its contents on the couch and on the low table in front of her: not only dried herbs, roots, bulbs, pieces of fragrant wood, little bottles with liquids, oils, the 'very best' rose water, all the ingredients for amber balls, for dried scents, incense, medicines, but also shells, pieces of coral, rare stones, little jewels, curiosities, and what not.

A ring cut from a white marble-shell with black inlay; a dried lobster claw which looked exactly like a little swan; a bracelet of scarlet shells for men to wear to war. And also really precious things like the horn of a rhinoceros; a Stone of Life (all metals melted together); a coconut from the Palm of the Sea, and such. She asked exorbitant prices for these, she would rather not sell them; she brought them along to be admired. The grandmother clapped her hands in proper astonishment and nodded, and nudged Felicia to do the same, and then proceeded with the business at hand.

The scales were brought; at times the grandmother tasted something for its genuineness, smelled it—it was an endless bargaining. Yet it was as if the two old women knew in advance what would be bought and how much would be paid for it. The grandmother put aside the things she was going to keep, 'get me my purse, granddaughter!' There was always just about the right amount of money in the purse.

The bibi carefully packed everything up again, in rags,

in boxes, little bags—some of the things were on no account to touch each other!—put it all back into the basket.

More coffee was brought for her and sweets; the bibi got up, put a tight dark hand on her stomach and said that she was completely satisfied; the grandmother escorted her to the top of the stairs—never farther—their hands touched each other.

The two little boys who had been kept away by Sjeba came running to see if something beautiful had been bought for the curiosities collection. Sjeba shook out the couch cover, the table cloth, beat up the pillows. 'Thank goodness!' she said to Felicia with a suppressed fury in her voice—was it fury or something else?

Felicia looked at her, 'yes, thank goodness,' she said too, and knew at once what the 'something else' was. Sjeba was afraid of the bibi, as she was herself.

On occasion, when the grandmother left them alone together, the bibi could look at her as if—with those gleaming black eyes, deeply sunk in the dark-brown face, sharp like awls and at the same time mortally tired—did she want to say something? what did she want to say? North America?, South America?, is he still alive?—no, he is not —and Felicia became deadly cold in the look from those eyes.

She was always glad when her grandmother came back.

Every now and again the bibi brought 'jewelry' with her. Once she had pushed a bound-up piece of cloth toward Felicia, with pearls in it.

Felicia, who usually did not care for jewelry, suddenly wanted those pearls—she was aware of nothing but their smoothness, their roundness, their gleam. She gave a start when the grandmother took the cloth out of her hands and handed it back to the bibi.

'Take these pearls from the sea back, and see that they are all there!' the grandmother said.

'Yes,' said the bibi, but she did not start to count the pearls, she kept her eyes on Felicia. 'They are beautiful,' she said softly, almost without moving her lips, and made a little gesture at her neck, 'beautiful for a string around the neck—for a lady, a gentleman likes—'

'Yes!' said the grandmother, 'very beautiful, wrap them up again, and in the future you must never bring pearls from the sea here, to the Small Garden, and do not forget that, bibi!'

All went awkwardly the rest of that day; for the first time Felicia had the feeling that her grandmother was a bothersome old woman who interfered in everything. She, Felicia, was no longer a child, she did most of the work; they earned a decent amount of money—if she wanted to buy pearls for a necklace, then what!

That evening when they were alone she took up the subject once more.

The grandmother said, 'pearls from the sea are tears, granddaughter!' (Why did she keep saying pearls from the sea?)

'I don't believe in that sort of thing,' Felicia said shortly —her voice was as hard as that of her mother.

'No, granddaughter, I know that.'

'You yourself always buy Arabian incense, that's tears too! at least that is what you have told me.'

The old woman started to laugh, 'but you're foolish, sweet granddaughter, pearls of the sea are tears we will have to cry ourselves, and the others are tears which were once cried for us people by the prophet Mohammed—that's what they say, at least, and that is not the same thing.'

On the next visit of the bibi—there was a long time in between—it happened again, in a way.

When the old woman was alone with Felicia she handed her a box made of folded palm leaves, in which there was a string of beads.

Felicia had never seen such beads before, neither of glass nor of metal, not of jade either, she thought; of stone or baked clay, rather, opaque, in mysteriously tender and quenched colors: orange, ocher, golden brown, some touched with black; so subdued of hue—melancholy almost, as if there was something of autumn in that little box woven from leaves, something of passing and dying.

She looked at them and held her breath.

'They are beautiful,' the bibi said, again in that soft toneless voice.

'Yes,' Felicia said and looked around to see where her grandmother was, 'yes, I want to buy them from you, how much do they cost, how much are they?'

'They are very expensive,' the bibi said softly, but she did not say how expensive.

But it was already too late, the grandmother had returned, like the first time she took the box from Felicia's hands, put the top on and gave it back. 'True,' she said, 'very expensive, for two of these one could formerly buy a human being, isn't that so, bibi?' And when the bibi did not answer, 'so you have not been able to remember that you weren't to bring pearls to the Small Garden?'

Felicia shook off her thoughts.

'Pearls! Are these pearls?' She looked furiously at her grandmother.

'Are these pearls, bibi?' asked the grandmother.

And the bibi muttered, scarcely audible, 'wrong pearls: pearls from the earth,' and stared fixedly at the ground in front of her.

With a jolt Felicia pushed back her chair, got up, walked away without saying a word. She went around the house and into the wood, sat down on the edge of the cistern and cried—she who never cried—what was there to cry for? there was nothing to cry for; she did not want to cry—he there—where?—she here, and it was autumn and life was going by . . .

Only days later, at the bay in the evening, the grandmother said musingly, as she had a way of doing, 'it is a pity you forgot to say goodbye to the bibi that time, she is offended now; did you like the beads? those beads are dug up from old graves, that is why they are called pearls from the earth, not from the sea—the wrong pearls; they have already been buried with somebody once. It isn't that they necessarily bring ill luck, oh no, some people say the opposite, that they bring good luck, and they like to have them because they think they're beautiful—you too, don't you, granddaughter? But then, they have already been buried once with somebody, perhaps you would not be able to forget that—the pearls from the sea in the sea, the pearls from the earth in the earth, better leave it that way.'

Felicia did not know what to answer except yes.

And much later again, in the time that Himpies was

going to be seven years old and ready for school, it happened with the shell strings; that was the end of the bibi.

Felicia and her grandmother had been busy in the garden, they had forgotten that the bibi was coming that morning, and when the old woman remembered she cried, 'go quickly, quickly!'

The bibi was already there. She was not sitting on the couch but on the edge of the side gallery, close to the pillar where the grandmother often sat at night; her legs were dangling over the garden—the two children were with her.

Himpies stood closest to her, he was almost in her lap and she held her basket in front of him. On top a string of gleaming white shells was lying, 'porcelana shells.' Some other strings the child had taken out and wound around himself: one was wound loosely around his neck a few times, the other all around his arm from the shoulder to the hand, still another he held up with both hands—the long white string hung in an arc, almost touching the ground. He was wearing only a little white shirt and white underpants; he was very tanned, not dark brown, a light goldish brown; his hair bleached almost yellow, much too long, combed stiffly down on both sides of his face like a page boy's.

He did not look left or right, stood completely motionless, silent, with wide-open eyes, frightened and delighted at once—entranced by the splendor of the gleaming shell strings around him.

On one side the dark bent old woman, repeating softly, beautiful, beautiful, beautiful; behind him his friend Domingoes in a dark-blue playsuit who watched and called to him from time to time, 'Himpies, don't do it! don't do it!'—all against the background of huge green trees and the flickering bright blue of the bay in the sun.

Felicia had not noticed her grandmother, who had come through the outbuildings and the passageways, who was now standing behind the bibi in her old garden slippers, her wrinkled sarong and jacket; she looked very tired, very pale, and she stared as did Felicia at the child in his attire.

'Himpies, take those strings off! they are not yours, you must give them back immediately to the—peddler woman'; she enunciated each word distinctly and she said 'peddler woman'—and that was the bibi!

The bibi had remained seated with her back toward the grandmother and now, without a word, she accepted the strings which the child handed to her slowly and unwillingly. The grandmother clapped her hands, called 'Sjeba!', and Sjeba, tall and thin and untidily dressed, came running, came down the stairs from the outbuilding, through the garden toward the children; she pretended not to see the bibi.

'Take our children along, Sjeba, make Himpies wash his hands in the bathroom, scrub them with soap!'

'Yes, sure, old mistress,' Sjeba said with a loud voice.

'See to it that the rowers and the helmsman have something to eat and to drink, and have them told that when they're rested they can take—' would she again say 'peddler woman'?—'take her back.'

'Yes, sure, old mistress,' Sjeba said again, she took Himpies and Domingoes each by a hand and pulled them along with her—Himpies looked back once.

When they had gone the bibi turned to the grandmother but remained seated with the basket in her lap, 'the child liked the shells, he wanted to play with them,' she said with that coaxing voice in which there was yet something of a threat, 'the mother of the child saw it and said nothing.' The grandmother did not let her finish, 'the child is still a small child,' she said shortly, 'and foolish, the mother is also still young and she has not been here for long, she is foolish too, but you and I, we are old and no longer foolish. We know—we have been taught—or aren't these the shell strings for the Mountain Alfuras of Ceram, for when they go head-hunting, when they lie in wait behind trees and shoot with arrows, when so much blood flows over the earth—' she took another step toward the bibi—'and you dare bring those shell strings here, here in my garden, to me, a white woman, a Christian woman, to our children here, who are Christian children who have done harm to no one—everyone has his own place, to each his own, that we know, you and I, that we have been taught! Or don't you know that yet? Haven't you been taught that?'

The bibi put her basket down beside her and got up; she stood in the garden, leaned on her knees against the edge of the gallery, turned her head toward the grandmother, stretched out both hands—'I ask forgiveness, madam,' she said.

'You'd better go ask the Mountain Alfuras of Ceram for forgiveness, and the little child here,' the grandmother said.

But she made her come up and sit on the couch, got coffee and sweets, took her purse and put five guilders on the table, 'so that you won't have a loss today,' she said, 'for I am tired, I want to go and rest.' She hesitated a moment, then added 'too bad that you are going on a journey, bibi, that you won't be able to come to the Small Garden any more.'

The bibi immediately took this up and wailed, 'Yes! on such a very long journey! only the Lord Allah knows whether I'll ever return from such a long journey.'

The grandmother kept looking at her—would she bid her goodbye after all those years? shake hands? Slowly she shook her head, turned and started toward her room, 'granddaughter,' she said, 'will you come with me and help me?' She had never asked that before.

Felicia went along with her; the bibi was left alone in the side gallery, she drank her coffee, ate the sweets, took the money, repacked her basket, went down the stairs toward the beach and climbed into the proa. After a while the rowers came, and the helmsman who pushed the boat off.

When they rowed away someone gave one ringing blow on the slave bell which resounded for a long time over the inner bay—Sjeba!

After that there was the crash of breaking china: the plate, the cup and the saucer.

'She doesn't drink from our things, we not from hers!' Sjeba came to announce around the corner of the door, and vanished again. Felicia looked at her grandmother to see her reaction: she was so careful with things. The old woman thought for a moment. 'Very good is Sjeba, granddaughter,' she said.

HIMPIES

· I ·

AND SO the bibi would not come back to the Small
Garden with her pearls from the sea and from the earth,
the scents of 'Happy Arabia' and the congealed tears of
the prophet.

The old goldsmith left too; his discontented young wife
finally won that battle. He took his brazier with him, his
bellows, his models: a pomegranate, a snail's head and
tail; and also his little son Domingoes.

Himpies cried his first real tears.

The grandmother decided that this was the moment to
stop selling 'the other things': medicines, scents, amber
balls. They could go on making the bracelets against rheumatism, but without the gold decoration (after all, gold
was not so very good for rheumatism), and send them di-
rectly to those who put in their orders by mail. And for
the rest, they would supply only the two hotels and the
military hospital: milk, eggs, fruits and vegetables—no
pickles, no mussel sauces, 'then we are no longer real
tradeswomen, granddaughter, then they can't tease Himpies about us in school.'

And in time the letter, the one letter, also came.

Felicia's father had written it: the 'legal counsel' of her
mother had started all over again with his search and
this time he had found a trail—not America, but the south
of France, on the other side of Marseille, the cheap side,

88

toward Spain. The man himself had not been found, for he had died there some years earlier, of pneumonia. At first he had had a bit of money, the landlady at his last boardinghouse had related, but that had run out—rather lonely, not very happy—a death certificate was enclosed and her father had written in the corner of his letter R. I. P., in three capitals.

Felicia and her grandmother were sitting together on the couch in the side gallery, sorting out the mail: thirty *Locomotives* (a whole month of the Java daily paper), two *Gracieuses* (the fashion magazine from Holland), and orders for bracelets, a few letters.

Felicia had read her letter—not far away then, not to America, not to North America nor to South America, just around the corner had been far enough, the stolen Snake with the Carbuncle Stone in his hand, and without having seen the child, and at the same time rather lonely, not very happy—she stared at that R. I. P., had her father liked him too then? She would have to show the letter to her grandmother or tell her—no, that she couldn't do. She could not listen to what she would say: 'such a pity, granddaughter,' or 'perhaps it's better this way; now when they ask Himpies in school about his father he will not have to lie' or 'it won't make Himpies very sad, you mustn't forget that he has never seen him' or (she wouldn't say it but she would think it) 'who is to blame? did your mother, with all her money . . . ?' and 'well, it is all over, for him too, if we only remain proud people, sweet granddaughter'—oh, she couldn't!

Yet her grandmother had to know; she pushed the letter toward her.

The old woman took the two sheets out of the envelope and read them: the note from 'my son Willem' and the death certificate and once more the note, put the sheets back into the envelope and gave it to Felicia; she sat still for a moment, huddled, nodded a few times without looking at Felicia, stared ahead with eyes as darkly tired as those of the bibi, not saying a word—outside, the trees, the inner bay, the sky—everything—the world—'yes,' she said then, 'yes, granddaughter,' and nothing else.

That was even worse.

The following week Felicia took Himpies to the town at the outer bay, to the schoolteacher's house where he would live. On Saturday afternoons after school he could come home with the milk proa and go back early Monday morning.

The town at the outer bay now dropped the 'young' in front of her name and called her 'the lady of the Small Garden'—as if that were a different person. And she was different: her husband dead, and her child no longer living with her in the same house.

It was all different: nothing was tugging at her any more, there were no possibilities, no choices. It was all here and now, except one thing: she would see to it that her son Himpies had a decent education, arms against life, boots and spurs, a helmet and a shield; money is still a strong shield!

So instead of taking it a little easier now, she started all kinds of enterprises. She sent for young cattle from Bali, the livestock had to be improved; she ordered seeds and cuttings from everywhere, asked advice from the Government Agricultural Service, planted new fruit trees, vegetables and also flowers. She tried to grow rice in the Garden—it didn't work; then she started to plant the hills with coco palms—that did work.

The grandmother didn't protest, she helped her where she could but she did not say much. The servants—there were more and more servants at the Garden—did say things —that eternal rushing and pushing! Especially Sjeba; she had adopted the habit of staring into space at each new request by Felicia, frowning angrily and drawling 'why,' a long drawn-out 'whyyyy?'

In addition to all that Felicia occupied herself more than ever with the child; during the week she again went regularly to the town and came to the school to get him, asked him what he had learned.

But school learning alone is not sufficient. She practiced for hours on her piano so that she could teach him well, she sang songs with him at the piano, and she wanted him to learn to play the bamboo flute.

Books were ordered to read from; and she told him all the stories she had been told, also the stories of the island.

In the town he had to go with her to see the Frenchman who had the collection of butterflies and insects— trays and trays full of brilliant color.

And also the old recluse who had the largest coral collection in the Moluccas; he made landscapes from it with rocks and stones, gnarled pieces of wood, whitened bones of animals, everything that washes ashore on a beach. He did not like to show them to anyone—but if the lady from the Small Garden insisted . . .

Then all that had to make way for the curiosities cabinet: Himpies should have the most beautiful, the largest collection of shells in the Moluccas, for now and for later!

It even involved the bibi.

One day the steersman of the milk proa brought a piece of cloth with a shell in it, 'from the bibi, a present for the boy Himpies and to ask forgiveness,' he said.

The grandmother was holding it irresolutely—Himpies wasn't there—but when Felicia saw it, she cried, 'Grandmother! I think that is the "Amoret Harp," that is a very rare one, rarer even than the "double Venus-heart" ' and she immediately went to look it up in Mr. Rumphius's book.

It was the Amoret Harp.

'What should we do with it?' the grandmother asked.

'Do!' said Felicia, 'nothing, put it in the drawer of the cabinet.'

'I'm not sure, granddaughter,' said the grandmother.

She wanted Felicia at least to find out how much the shell was worth. That was not difficult: Felicia was constantly buying and trading shells in those days.

The Amoret Harp was a very expensive shell.

The grandmother wrapped money in a piece of paper and put it in a box with some jars of candied fruits and gave it to the steersman—a present for the bibi in return, and to thank her—that was what he should say. She did not invite the bibi back to the Garden.

In that way the Amoret Harp found its place in the top drawer.

Every new shell was immediately looked up in Rumphius: what kind, family, class? The Latin names were too difficult but Felicia thought that Himpies could learn the Dutch names by heart. From time to time, on Sundays, she opened the drawers, pointed them out and re-hearsed him; and when he made a mistake she became angry.

Once she bought a little shell which was called 'Cinderella.' She embroidered a story around it for Himpies which would help him to remember all the names—there were one hundred names of shells in the story. It started like this: once 'Cinderella' set out to find her prince. A 'white donkey' was waiting to carry her, for she did not know how far she would have to go. All kinds of animals and birds came with her: in front, a 'white tiger' and a 'yellow tiger' to clear the road for her, 'scorpions' and 'centipedes' and 'little snakes'; and around her head flew 'pigeons' and 'partridges'—and Felicia went on with a long list of shells that all had names of animals and birds.

'And Cinderella met a "prince's funeral,"' she said, 'but luckily enough it was not her prince who was being buried.

'After a time she found her own prince, and they went back together. First they gave presents to each other: she gave him an "elephant's tooth" and "onyx from the sea," and he gave her the "double Venus-heart." And she wore a "royal mantle," and he had a "green crown" on his head.

'And they did not want to live in a house together,' Felicia ended, 'but in a tower: that tower was called "Tour de Bra."'

She liked the story herself, she read it aloud and pointed out the shells as she went along. And when she had finished she saw how they looked at each other, the old great-grandmother and the young great-grandson, and they smiled, and did not say anything immediately. They liked it! They liked it that she, Felicia, liked it so, and had so much pleasure in the shells, and in all the weird names they had—and she realized that she should leave the child alone in the future.

He was an amenable child who wanted to obey; every Monday morning he went to the school in town without fussing—at the Small Garden there was no school, and a child has to go to school. He worked at his studies—not very hard, just enough to pass. But he did not want the other things—study piano, play the flute, sing songs—imagine! He did not like to be read to, he did not care for stuffed animals and coral landscapes and shells; how on earth could he remember all those names? He did like the curiosities cabinet, because it belonged to the Garden —and he loved the Garden.

He loved it in his own way—without much ado, as it was, as it had been for seven years for the two children Domingoes and Himpies. They had never just looked at it, they had never seen that the Garden was 'beautiful' and so terribly far away and quiet, they had not seen the fear in the Garden. Together they had never been afraid.

They had not believed in the terrible Leviathan; they had even plagued the coral fishers to bring in another one! The fishers hadn't, it would be a hard job and how much would it be worth to the old lady? Moreover two of those shells together would attract lightning.

They had helped dress and paint the palm-wine mannikin—a fresh rattan thorn straight through him—and when they were older it was they who always put him up in the palm trees. There was nothing more exciting than to climb the rattan rope ladder into a high tree and hide yourself in the green foliage, for hours.

The stories of the man with the blue hair about his son had not scared them either: the storming of a fort, the crackling of rifles (he could imitate that very well), fight, get wounded, die—his son was always being wounded, gravely wounded, lots of blood, he never died.

But dying was not something strange.

They had their own little graveyard in the woods for all the animals they had kept which had died: a wounded turtle that had lived on for a long time in a tub of sea water and had bitten their fingers when they fed it, a young deer, a cassowary chick which followed them every-where when they stamped hard on the ground as the mother cassowary does, and a lot of squirrels and birds—the black parrot with the lame leg had a mausoleum in the middle of the cemetery.

Every day they passed the graves at the edge of the wood; they knew all about the three girls who had been given poison to drink—they understood quite well: some-one who drinks poison, or is stabbed with a knife, or is shot with a rifle or with arrows, dies, is murdered—they knew all that.

They also knew about funerals.

In those years old Sarah and Eliah died within a few hours of each other, in the night.

They were washed, dressed neatly and laid in the cof-fins, the grandmother put in strongly scented herbs, cam-phor wood and sandalwood, sprinkled aromatic oil, and gave some of her best sheets to cover the dead—then the family could come, the others who lived at the Garden, people from the village; also the schoolteacher who led the prayers. They sang psalms—perhaps they would rather have sung the old lament of the 'hundred things'—oh, soul—and called ee-ee-ee-ee-ee. But the schoolteacher said, the Lord gave and the Lord hath taken away.

Himpies and Domingoes had not seen that part of it. Later they were present and saw the men prepare the proas by torchlight, carry the coffins out and put them in the gala proa under the little roof on which the gong-players would sit. Large winged proas were waiting on the beach for all who would come along; burials at the Garden were not permitted any more, they had to go to one of the graveyards near the town at the outer bay.

They waited for the dawn, not the sunrise—the sky showed a touch of gray, the inner bay beneath it another, more tender shade of grayness, the trees seemed even darker than usual with their heavy wet foliage—and then a small procession of women came out from under the trees toward the beach. They were all dressed in the same severely pleated black skirts and long-sleeved jackets, in one hand the little Bible and the large folded white handkerchief, and in the other their Sunday slippers with curled points which must not get wet when they climbed into the proas.

Sjeba the daughter-in-law went in front; there were more women like her, tall and bony; they all walked slowly and solemnly and with great dignity, as if they were carrying something else in their hands besides the Book, the handkerchief and the slippers—something about the secret of life and death.

As soon as they were on board the proas sailed, the gala proa with the dead going first; the gong players beat a muted rhythm for the rowers, the steersman stood upright in the stern.

The grandmother stayed behind at the Garden with the two children. First she stood on the beach watching the boats cross the inner bay; she cried for a moment, wiped her eyes and said, 'goodbye, have a good journey!' and to the boys, 'you must say the same.' The two children repeated her words.

After that she walked to the slave bell; she did not pull the rope but took a wooden pestle from the kitchen, wound a piece of cloth around it, and beat with it on the bronze, slowly and regularly. It sounded like a church bell. The children were standing, one on each side of her. They stayed near her that day and didn't run away as they were wont to do.

But in those days the two boys had been together at the Small Garden; now the child Himpies was there alone.

Domingoes went to another school in the town, and at first he occasionally came for the weekend; but then the old goldsmith and his young wife moved even farther away, to her island, no one knew where.

After that Dutch children from Himpies' class came to stay at the Garden during the weekends, but the Garden was not very friendly to the new children. They got sunburned, fell from trees, bruised their feet on the coral; one stepped on a sea urchin.

Himpies was good friends with them but he didn't seem to care much whether they came with him to the Small Garden or not, and so after a while they stopped coming.

He learned to be alone at the Garden—sometimes he would stand, suddenly motionless, with his eyes wide open, and look and see that the Garden was beautiful. He now saw things separated from each other, one by one: one tree, one rock, one flower, one shell on the beach, one bird. At times he was afraid alone, but not very, and he did not know what it was that he feared.

Now he also went to sit and talk with the 'adults,' looked at them; and everyone liked to have the boy Himpies sit with them and look at them—the people in the village across the river, the servants in the Garden, his other mother Sjeba, his great-grandmother, his mother Felicia too. With her he did not have long conversations; they loved each other but the child could not cope with her vehemence and her quickly aroused irritation. Already then, when he was still in elementary school, he began saying what he would often say later—'well, yes, certainly, Mrs. Small Garden'—and then he would look at her intently and smile, and the lady of the Small Garden never answered.

When he had finished grade school Felicia sent him to Java, to a secondary school in Surabaya; he again boarded with a teacher. Once a year during the summer holiday he could come home for some weeks—the voyage was a long and very expensive one.

After his third year Felicia pronounced it all nonsense, she said it would be much better if he went straight to Holland for the last two years; that way he could make friends for his university days.

Himpies looked at her and asked, 'for how long?'

'Do you mean how long will you stay in Holland? Long!

Two years of secondary school, perhaps three—you always lose time when you change, six years to become a doctor if you work really hard, one year, or say two, at a university in France or Germany, to specialize—better everything at once, then you are somebody.' And without sparing his feelings or her own: 'three and six and two, that is eleven—eleven years.'

'No,' said the boy, 'that is impossible, that is too long.'

'Too long!' Felicia snapped, 'too long to learn a decent profession! What do you want then? Are you too much of a slacker to study? Oh, I know, you'd rather hang around on the Small Garden. Go native, walk around in a pajama, sell eggs and milk, and spices which nobody wants any more! Shop around for a woman with some money, I guess—she had almost said 'sugary money'—'otherwise a plate of sago with a fried fish from the bay; is that what you want?'

'We don't live on sago with a fried fish from the bay.'

Then Felicia explained to him the way they had earned their money, especially in the beginning, by peddling 'the other things' in the Chinese and Arab quarters; she told him everything. 'And only because great-grandma made them—when she is no longer here they won't even buy a rheumatism bracelet from me, you watch! Too long, what do you mean too long? You are still very young, Himpies.'

He looked around him as if he were searching for something, did not know what to say—'then I won't see great-grandma again.'

'No, of course not,' said Felicia, 'she is past eighty, that is very old for the tropics,' and more softly than she usually spoke, 'we all die, Himpies, and we receive nothing for nothing.'

The boy regarded her again, 'and you? and mother Sjeba? and all the others? and the Small Garden?' he asked, stammering for a moment.

'Oh,' she said. 'You should trust us to last a little longer —the Garden will, anyway.'

Then he smiled, just vaguely. 'Well, yes, certainly, Mrs. Small Garden,' he said, but the brown eyes with the little spots looked past her.

· II ·

WHEN HIMPIES had been gone for two years the grandmother died; she was not very ill beforehand—sometimes it seemed as if she had lost all her certainties toward the end of her life.

She seldom used the word 'proud' any more.

Once she said to Felicia, 'when I'm gone you must move everything from the "special drawer" into a drawer of Himpies' cabinet, but without the little sentinels—you would forget to change them anyway, granddaughter, because you don't believe in them.'

Felicia laughed, 'but do you, really?' and she had answered, 'I don't quite know; you must remember, I've been alone at the Garden for so many years, alone with the servants—Sarah was my friend—she believed in them, and I . . . I liked to believe in them too.'

She missed the boy and often asked for him, 'why isn't

Himpies here? where is Himpies?' and then she remembered that he was studying to be a doctor, 'he can have my snakestone, don't forget! When he has used it he must put it in milk to extract the venom—' she stopped suddenly—'don't you believe in the snakestone either, granddaughter?'

She could get restless; 'is there still not enough money? why does Himpies have to become an army surgeon, in a uniform?' and she calmed down only when Felicia explained that there was enough money for him to study medicine properly, at the university, that he was certainly not going to become an army surgeon such as they had in the garrison in the town.

'That is good, granddaughter, don't let Himpies put on a uniform.'

Once more she talked about the three little girls, 'you mustn't forget the three girls, granddaughter—forgetting is not good,' and she muttered something about the slave girl—the years of the slaves—'not so long ago, granddaughter.'

And then she said, 'my mother came from here, a child of the island, perhaps she came from here, from the Small Garden, and perhaps her mother—I don't know,' and she shook her head.

On one of her last days she called all the servants to her, one at a time, some people from the village too, and gave each a souvenir; afterward she said to Felicia with a little gesture, as if she were handing her something, 'the Small Garden is for you, granddaughter. It isn't that I forget my son Willem—I love my son very much,' and she enumerated the names of all those whom she had loved most during her life, 'and my husband and my father and mother and the sisters all four, and you, sweet granddaughter, and Himpies'—it was as if she wanted to say more but she was tired and fell asleep; a little later she died, very quietly, in the night.

In the morning in the gray dawn they carried her away; everyone came along. When they sailed off in the proas Felicia remembered too late that nobody had stayed behind to say goodbye, have a good journey, and to ring the slave bell. The grandmother dead, and where were the children?

Now began one of the hardest times in her life.

She was worried about Himpies: he was boarding again with a teacher who had a large family, with other student boarders, and little time; Himpies himself wrote irregularly, sometimes not for months. He was living in the same town in Holland where her parents had stayed after the sugar market crashed. Her mother began to ail, and wrote her long confused letters full of complaints; her father wrote regularly, very briefly, there wasn't much in his letters: young Willem was a nice fellow, she shouldn't worry, he would make his way, and many greetings.

The Garden was there, but submerged in its greenness; Sjeba was grumpy, and didn't speak much. At times there was nothing but the deep humming silence around her—not even the sound of water and wind and trees, and no voices.

The work remained, and the money. She worked hard, earned much. When her mother died there was more money than anyone had thought—she inherited it together with her father.

The lady of the Small Garden is rich, the town at the outer bay said.

In those days she began making expeditions all over the island. As soon as she was on the road she felt better, in a proa, or rather, walking, climbing in the mountains, over rocks and cliffs; nothing was too steep or too far. She bathed and swam in every clear stream she crossed.

She did not go alone; Sjeba started by asking 'why' but came along in the end, also some older men from among the servants—one with a rifle. Sometimes they visited places where they should not have been.

On those trips she also began to hunt for antiques: old china and porcelain, furniture, crystal—everything. She took medicines with her, as her grandmother had taught her, and money. She was never afraid. Everyone knew her: the little white woman, the lady from the inner bay, a bit stocky, on sandals, in a simple skirt and jacket, with curly brown hair; behind her, three from the island: Sjeba, tall and lanky, two elderly men in black, one with the rifle, the other with an old brown bag full of medicines, food, clean clothes, and the gray purse with the silver lock.

The house on the Garden was being filled with beautiful things: long racks of china along the walls, *famille verte* and *famille rose;* water pitchers with dragons' or lions' heads, black carved furniture, sometimes with inlay, brass, tin.

Into the guest room went a four-poster of black wood with a gilded pineapple on each corner post.

Felicia did not want to change the house in any way, but she did have the living room extended with an archway and stairs leading to a large verandah facing the lemon orchard, with a pond on each side filled by the stream from the wood—on the surface lotus flowers floated. The cistern had to stay the way it was.

There was plenty of time for building: not even four of the eleven years had passed.

But when Himpies was in his first year at the university he wrote her that he did not want to continue his studies, that he wanted to go to the military academy and become an officer—that did not take so long—he hoped that she would approve.

Felicia sat down on the edge of the side gallery with the letter in her hand and leaned against a pillar. What could she do? Go there, take him by the hand, make him continue those long years of study he did not want? Leave the Garden?—that would be the end of it! She saw the empty space in front of her where the old house had been—it was still almost bare—saw all the other things, saw all the sadness, and it was as if it took a solid shape and threw a shadow over the Garden.

She jumped up and went inside to write him an answer: he should follow his own heart; and then went on to tell him little things about the Garden which she knew he would like to hear.

· III ·

FELICIA AND SJEBA were standing under the plane trees at the beach; all the others kept in the background—they were a bit afraid of the lady from the Small Garden but they were curious—again nobody remembered in time to ring the slave bell.

Felicia would not say, 'there you are!' and 'I have been waiting for you!' as her grandmother had once; she could not say anything: the tall, the handsome stranger from the hotel in Nice, in a white uniform, stepped out of the proa and came toward her—and her heart stopped beating.

But when he was close, it was someone else, with other eyes, the warm brown eyes with spots of the boy Himpies, and he said, 'hello, mother, there you are, I'm finally back!' and embraced her; and 'hello, mother Sjeba, you're still here, how lucky that you're still here!' embraced her, ran to the others, shook all their hands, patted them on the shoulders and looked at them and laughed and repeated, 'here I am again!' and 'are you still here!' and 'how lucky you're still here!' to all and everyone and everything, and laughed—and wanted to know all at once: how was Felicia? and the Garden? and the coco palms? and the cows and the milk and the eggs? 'can you still manage, mother?' and 'great-grandma gone, I told you so! are you still making bracelets? why not let me help—are the parakeets dead too? where do I sleep? how are they in the village, the old man with the blue hair? has his son taken another fort by storm? where on earth is Domingoes? I'm going to track him down one of these days! are you sleeping in great-grandma's room now? is everything unchanged there? where did you get all these beautiful things?'

He looked at the curiosities cabinet, opened the top drawer of the Cinderella story, immediately picked out the Amoret Harp, 'what's-its-name again—the bibi gave it to me! you must tell me that story again about Cinderella and her prince, they didn't live in a house but in a tower, the . . . no, don't say it, I know—the Tour de Bra, wasn't it?'

Felicia opened another drawer, in which the 'treasure' was laid on a piece of Palembang silk, and he asked, 'why did you do that? and without the sentinels of Good Fortune? does great-grandma approve?' and laughed, and 'does no one know where Domingoes has gone?' and at times he hummed snatches from the only Malayan song he had ever been able to remember.

'And everything is still here!' and he threw back his head and laughed, and looked. He had to see the new verandah and the two lotus ponds—when he saw the beautiful four-poster with the golden pineapples in the guest room he whistled and said, 'well, yes, certainly, Mrs. Small Garden!' and looked at her closely and laughed aloud.

Later he calmed down. They were having tea together at the inner bay, and it seemed to Felicia that he had not changed much, perhaps he was a little gayer than before—that could also be the excitement; friendly to everyone, he had always been that, and at the same time a bit absent, he still had that about him. When she asked him something he would wait a moment as if he had not heard, and then he might answer a hesitant yes, and—yes and no . . .

'Why haven't you brought grandfather with you?'

'Yes, we did discuss it, but I think he couldn't quite muster the courage; perhaps if he could have taken grandma's little dogs along on the ship—grandfather is very nice, mother.'

'Yes,' Felicia said, 'he is.'

Had he not seen how spiritless and beaten the old man was after a lifetime with a nagging rich wife—or had her father always been like that?

'Was grandmother nice to you?'

He hesitated. 'Not so very nice,' he then said, 'I mean, not as nice as grandfather, but . . . she was so well-meaning, she always wanted to buy things for me.'

Felicia looked at him sideways—nice, and very nice, and not so very nice. Her son in a uniform; it became him well; why in a uniform? They had never been a family of officers. And suddenly she recalled grandmother's words, 'don't let Himpies put on a uniform'; would she tell him? no, it was too late now anyway.

He hummed a few notes, he couldn't get the tune out of his head, and stopped again; she always used to tell him not to hum.

'So I'm sleeping in the beautiful room? are you sure I should? with the three girls in pink—are they still there?'

'Yes, of course,' Felicia said.

She had given him the front room with the two large windows; his bed was pushed in front of them. She knew exactly what he would do: open the screens and blinds wide, so that he could lie on his bed under the mosquito curtain and look out under the trees, over the inner bay—the inner bay beneath the stars, the moonlight, storm, rain; lie and listen to the small surf and the wind in the trees. Even as a child he had never liked to sleep in a closed dark room.

When he went to bed that evening he was still whistling that song.

It was called Watching from a distance.

Had he been so unhappy in Europe?

· IV ·

SECOND LIEUTENANT HIMPIES stayed at the garrison in the town at the outer bay for a year and a half (that nice major of his had arranged that). Every leave he could get, almost every Sunday, he spent in the Small Garden at the inner bay; and he brought out all his colleagues and their wives by turns.

They were all young and nice—very nice, said Himpies; very new, Felicia thought them.

They called her 'Mother Small,' they came to sit and talk with her: about the slow promotions, and money troubles, about their babies, and sometimes about how they loved another man or woman more than their own; or that life was difficult, that they didn't like this island in the Moluccas very much (it was so far away and only one ship a month), that they longed so much for home, for Holland.

Afterward they bathed in the inner bay or in the cistern, had a picnic or walked in the hills all the way to the foot of the mountains. They sat around the large round table in the living room on the antique chairs and ate rijsttafel from the *famille verte* china with gold crests; next to the silver beside each plate lay a spoon of real Nautilus mother-of-pearl, for the strong mussel sauces, black or white. There was also a platter of roasted fish with ground kanari nuts, lemon and red peppers—very good!

In the evening there was dancing on the new verandah, and when the lemon trees were in bloom the air was drenched with the heavy sweet scent; she played the piano, Himpies was expert in leading the quadrille. There were Chinese lanterns in the trees and it was very gay at the Small Garden.

Between dances the couples went for walks along the beach; the young women carried fans, to cool themselves and their escorts, to whisper behind—the moon was shining.

Then Felicia played Chopin or Schubert, never a song of the island, never The evening is too long, my love, and the road too far; never The gong is calling from afar, from afar; not even Watching from a distance.

And there were other things which neither Felicia nor Himpies would ever talk about with these new people, no matter how nice they were: Martin the Portuguese sailor, the daughter of the Rajah, the Dancer with the Shell. Nor the man with the blue hair—he belonged to the boys Himpies and Domingoes together, like the Leviathan and the palm-wine mannikin. When their guests passed the three graves at the edge of the wood, mother and son answered any questions with 'oh, three children who died here in the Garden, a long time ago.'

And no matter how far they wandered through the woods and the hills, without Sjeba none of them would ever come upon the spring with the bitter water.

On those weekends the keys to the curiosities cabinet,

the books of Mr. Rumphius, were 'mislaid.' And who would ever think of talking to these new people about the coral woman in her flowery dress who had been loved by Mr. Rumphius?

Himpies' best friend at that time was a young medical officer—Bear, they called him—a giant with feet like canoes, big careful hands like shovels. He swore like a trooper, but to please Mother Small he watched his language when she was near, and only interjected after every few words, God have mercy on me, or something like that.

He was also most pronounced in his sympathies and antipathies: a woman was an angel from heaven, exquisite, or a mean shrew; a man a noble fellow or a miserable cad—there was nothing in between. Next to him Himpies sometimes seemed a bit faded, or was he? the brown eyes with the spots weren't faded.

Then there was in the town at the outer bay a young woman who never came to the Small Garden with the others—Felicia had never seen her, and she never would, but she had heard the others talk about her. The woman was also an officer's wife and she had a little daughter. Her husband was away on an expedition to New Guinea; that always took a long time. In the meanwhile she was preparing her departure. It was a bad marriage, the husband did not want to give her a divorce but had finally agreed to her going to live with her mother and taking the child along—her mother was Irish and lived somewhere in an Irish village in the middle of nowhere. There was very little money. The young woman wasn't hurrying to leave.

Bear in particular always talked about her: Toinette, that was her name, was everything at once: an angel from heaven, and exquisite too, with black hair and green eyes (you know, that's because of her Irish mother)—the little daughter Nettie even sweeter, even prettier, if such were possible, a very nervous child, Doctor Bear said worriedly, small wonder after all the unhappiness with the husband and father—that miserable cad! He went on and on about it; 'and when he finds out that there's someone else he'll certainly take the child away from her—' and here he suddenly fell silent, startled by his own words.

One Sunday evening before going to bed Felicia and her son were alone together in the living room; they were standing near the curiosities cabinet. Himpies opened the top drawer, he had a habit of doing that occasionally; he asked whether an acquaintance of his, a lady he knew— an officer's wife—could come and stay for some time at the Garden with her daughter: the child had just been ill—and he looked into his mother's eyes. She could never resist that, 'yes, all right,' she agreed curtly.

'Perhaps the child—her name is Nettie—' he smiled— 'will like the shells, the story of Cinderella, will you tell it to her?' and he looked in the red drawer with the pretty shells.

'Himpies,' said Felicia with her hard voice, 'don't start a perkara with a married woman: it only brings sadness, for everybody.'

She used the Malayan word *perkara*—a belittling word: 'a little affair.'

Himpies did not say anything at first, he stood near the red cabinet, tall and slim in his white uniform; he bent over the drawer, put in his hand, took out one of the shells, not the double Venus-heart but the Amoret Harp, held it against his ear—but the shell was so small, too small to carry the murmur of the sea, the murmur of the green, green sea; then he put the shell back among the others and closed the drawer.

'Well, yes, certainly, Mrs. Small Garden,' he said, nothing more, and he did not smile and did not look at her. Then he went to his bedroom.

When Felicia was lying in bed she thought, now he is lying there, so near, and he looks out through the window over the inner bay and is sad.

And in her bed in the town at the outer bay lies the young woman with the black hair and the green eyes, and she is sad; she will have taken the child into bed with her, holding it close; perhaps the child is sad too.

Somewhere on New Guinea in the jungle lies Bear's 'miserable cad' on an army cot—is he sad, or are miserable cads never sad?

And I'm lying here in my bed and am sad; I don't want to be, I've had enough sadness, I'm too old for it—and now they'll come here too!

But they did not come: that Thursday was the day when the one boat of the month sailed for Java and wherever you wanted to go from there, and with the boat the young woman Toinette and the child Nettie left, completely unexpectedly.

Bear came to tell her, he was almost in tears: 'Toinette gone like that, run away, and she knew that we were all . . . all behind her, and not a word, not a note!'

Oh, Felicia thought, a note—

'I don't like running away either,' she said, 'but what else could she have done? You said yourself that the man would take the child away if he heard that there was someone else."

Bear looked up at her.

'She must have told Himpies that she was leaving,' Felicia asked.

'By God, I don't know,' Bear answered, 'Himpies isn't saying anything.'

Then Felicia asked, 'how long has this been going on? Have they lived together all this time, do you think?'

Bear became angry, 'why do you ask me, Mother Small, you must ask Himpies if you want to know that. And anyway, do you think that would have been so wrong?'

'I didn't ask because I think it so wrong,' Felicia said.

They were both silent and then Bear said, 'there's one consolation, it was such a short time.'

Felicia did not answer, stared ahead—poor Bear! As if 'short' or 'long' made much difference.

After a while Himpies came back to the Garden, without saying anything; Felicia did not say anything either.

She had bought a large sailing proa for him, a seaworthy one; it was moored at a village on the other side of the isthmus, at the ocean beach—they could always get a crew there. Himpies and Bear began going on long cruises to the other islands; sometimes Felicia came along, but not often.

She knew that a bay and rocks and trees bending over the surf cannot relieve sadness—can sadness be relieved, or can one only pass it by, very slowly?

A day in the radiant sunlight and the sky's blue, in

the shadow of a proud dark sail, over rustling waves, along new coastlines, wouldn't that help to get past sadness?—for a while, for that one day at least.

Bear was transferred.

And then Himpies was sent on an expedition, taking the place of a fellow officer who had fallen ill—just a small expedition, on Ceram, quite near: a show of strength for the Mountain Alfuras who had become a nuisance and who were going on too many head-hunts.

· v ·

FELICIA WAS on her way back from the town in the empty milk proa—there was mail, a letter from Himpies. He wrote seldom and then suddenly a very long letter about anything and everything; sometimes he numbered the paragraphs as if to keep things straight for himself.

First: who do you think is here! I found Domingoes again, after almost twenty years (well, Mr. Himpies, it isn't quite that long); sometimes, to everyone's delight, he says tuan Himpies instead of tuan Lieutenant, but never without the tuan; why not?

He is now our universally respected sergeant!

You don't know how nice he is. As a matter of fact, I don't think he has changed at all, he is rather serious, reserved—but I always remembered him that way. Does a splendid job, popular with the men and yet severe. 'Listen!' he says, 'the beginning of it all is to listen!' Isn't that funny—think of it. Domingoes!

On Sundays he preaches in the church for the native

troops; I went once. He preaches well, a bit gloomily, like a prophet, I'd say, or is it just the solemnity of the Malayan? His text was from Isaiah, about 'the islands': Keep silence before me, oh islands; the isles saw it and feared; the ends of the earth were afraid, drew near, and came.

Do you know it? Isn't it beautiful? That 'islands' bound us all together.

Second: a word about the others here, the C.O.: a captain, not so very nice, a bit standoffish, hasn't even sniffed the islands yet, thinks that the lieutenant shouldn't be too chummy with the sergeant because 'familiarity breeds contempt,' that's how it looks to him.

The doctor (nice) does try to get a whiff of the islands; he is always fishing, collects shells and coral and is interested in 'magic.' He does not approve of this expedition at all: head-hunting means the collecting of 'soul material' for the community, the young men who are coming of age. What business is it of ours to poke our blunt Western noses into that?

The good doctor cooled off a bit the other day when we brought back a bunch of freshly cut heads from a mountain village, left behind in haste by the Alfuras who had gone still higher into the mountains.

Poor heads, not only of grownups, but also of children, some rather small children I think: going out to play in the fields, away from the village—and then the warriors of the other village, from behind the trees—

These warriors are beautiful, the doctor says (he has it from a book), in their ritual trappings, naked, with a belt of milk-white tree bark around their loins, their hair bound high over a coco shell or a piece of wood, with feathers from a bird of paradise, and on top of it all a crown of white shells—gleaming white porcelana shells, as big as eggshells. And a string of them around the neck, some large yellow rings through the ears, green plumes made of leaves on arms and legs.

I'm quite ready to believe that they are beautiful; I would like to meet one, but with me in war trappings too. And I do think they should be cured of their habit of hunting heads, magic or no magic.

Third: to get back to the barracks, I can't even begin to tell you about our men and about the chain gang, except for one fellow who, for heaven knows what reason, has developed a tender affection for your son Himpies.

He is a mass-murderer. A complicated story: he got some half-witted woman to put arsenic in the coffee at a wedding party because he wanted to revenge himself on one of the guests. A considerable number of the guests turned up their toes, and it came out that the arsenic was his; he would have had to be hanged so many times that they somehow decided to put him away for life instead. He is a shriveled old man now, but very strong, I think, especially his hands—although he didn't do it with them. When I look at him sometimes he makes me shiver.

Whenever we're in the field he takes care of me in a touching way, he would like to clear the whole jungle, look behind every tree, smooth all the paths for me, and they are quite some paths. Doesn't that put your mind at ease about me?

Fourth: I left so hastily, and there are always things we would have liked to say but somehow didn't.

Of course I should not have become an officer. I'm especially sorry for you, because you didn't like it at all, I realize that. And for myself? Well, I'm still young, perhaps you'll help me once more. It is the same with Toinette; as long as the child is so small she has to stay with her, of course, but she is still young too, perhaps there's time, perhaps there are still possibilities for us. I could get out of the army, go to an agricultural college, learn to plant palms, and then we'll come and live at the Garden together.

But it's all far off and I cannot make it come very much closer.

And then there's this, to use an expression Domingoes has for it: 'I'll say I'm content.' That's what we all feel here, for the time being at least: contentment with our community, this community of men without women, fighters in our way.

Including me! Content with Domingoes in the first place, with the soldiers, even with the captain and the doctor, and the faithful mass-murderer, content also with this island, again an island and a beautiful one, but so different; even the surf from the open sea is different from our little hop-scotch surf in the inner bay, with its steadily repeating equally heavy beats when the tide is coming in. I am still not used to it, but it is nice to fall asleep to.

Domingoes and I had a talk about you some days ago: he has the greatest admiration for you (does he really remember, or do people talk so much about you?), the way the lady of the Small Garden cooks, even better than her grandmother, your kanari cake, your mussel sauces, how efficient you are, ready to handle anything: what are the facts? do this or that; no fussing, somebody to count upon.

That's how you are. I'm not like that; mother, am I a weakling? Everything is so relative in my mind. Of course, I see good and bad, and try to stick to the good in my own way, but I think that making judgments is very difficult. And what befalls us, life itself, I'd say, everything, long or short, nice or miserable, shouldn't we accept it as it falls without too much examination?

At times I think of great-grandma, who said: learn to be proud—if we only remain proud people. You thought that when she said 'proud' she meant 'courageous.' Yes and no, perhaps she really meant 'proud'? there is something in that word 'proud.' And also in that she did not let us use the word 'happy,' and in the sentinels of the drawer; was it wise to throw them away, the sentinels of good fortune? Oh, there are so many things I think of, but I'm stopping.

Take good care of yourself, I'm being taken care of by many here, your loving son H.

Then there was several postscripts: thank you for all the good things, the sauces, and all else; I share them with Domingoes.

You never told me about the three girls in pink, why not? Give them my greetings, and also to Mother Sjeba and all who in my thoughts belong together in the blessed Small Garden.

Felicia was sitting with the letter in her hands.

The sun was still shining but the mountains and hills and woods along the shore, seen from the proa here, were dark and still and drawn out into the distance, and so the inner bay seemed wider and more open than usual.

She had read the letter and was happy with it, and sad —pleased with his praise, sad that he was so far away.

She was thinking about him as so often: in one way he was far beyond his age, as if he were already prepared to give to the incomplete in his life its value and its place— to an unhappy love, for instance, the wrong profession, the things missed, lost, failed, and not only to Happiness, Success, Completion. But wasn't that for an older man, one who has been tried, who has learned his lessons?

And then suddenly his childish: 'I'll say I'm content'— was that childish?

Domingoes, sergeant and preacher, the stiff captain, the doctor with his interest in magic, the mass-murderer, the soldiers, a Mountain Alfura resplendent in his snowy white shell-string, the poor hunted heads, the surf, the Garden, his youth, the woman Toinette, a bottle of mussel sauce, the islands of Isaiah—was that, all added together, not a complete life?

The life we shouldn't try to examine too carefully—the proa suddenly lost speed, almost came to a stop.

What was it now?

Something had come loose on one of the wings, the steersman said, the rattan ropes had to be tightened, other-wise they might even capsize—it wouldn't take long.

Felicia looked annoyed—always something!—stared ahead, then over the edge of the proa into the water of the inner bay. There was no wind and the water was clear there, with green and blue discolorations, hardly moving, almost motionless—

Suddenly there were three young turtles, all three of the same size, their shields gleaming, almost pink, with a symmetrical pattern of dark brown and yellow and black stripes and spots; each with its four fins waving up and down, young and yet with the same old man's bald head on a wrinkled neck, with little gleaming eyes under sleepy lids and a large yellow beak like a bird's.

They let themselves drop, their fins upright, as if they were drowning, rose again; they kept together, swam over and under each other, carefully, not touching, with a strangely thoughtful and yet casual grace.

Then, as unexpectedly as they had risen, they dropped down into the deep and did not reappear.

Felicia looked ahead and without knowing it bent her head sideways and asked, 'content with the three young turtles—can one say that?'

'Come on, you! Get a move on!' the lady of the Small Garden called out with her hard voice, 'how long is this going to take? Don't you want to get home today? I do!'

When they landed the water was so still, not one ripple, that the trees, the white pavilion stood reflected in the inner bay—that happened very rarely.

The following day Felicia stayed at the Garden. Once or twice she went down to the beach, to stand under the plane trees for a moment.

Late in the afternoon a proa moored; visitors? She did not expect anyone. An officer, a high one, the major himself, the—very nice—major himself. He greeted her, sat down as if he had come for tea, did not say much, cleared his throat—he had come to say, to his great regret, a message had been received, her son had been shot from an ambush by a Mountain Alfura, with an arrow—he was wounded, badly wounded—

'You can tell me.'

'Yes,' he said then.

'When?' she asked, as if that made any difference.

'Yesterday afternoon,' said the major. The message had come by a courier proa, there were no details yet.

Yesterday afternoon, yesterday afternoon, that was when she had been looking at the three young turtles dancing in the water.

When the major got up she walked with him to the proa, thanked him for coming in person; after standing awhile at the inner bay she turned around, climbed up the stairs, through the side gallery and to the outbuildings.

Night had fallen.

In the large kitchen the hanging lamp was lit and some wall lamps, and it was crowded: all the servants, also the seasonal spice pickers, the rowers were there, and the women; from the village a raft was crossing with still more people—like the night she had arrived at the Small Garden with the child Himpies, and they had come to see him —thus they now came again for the one who was not there, and to wake with her through this night.

Now, as then, serious and silent and keeping in the background: because they did not matter, nor did Felicia; it was the child—her child, their children, the children of men—in life and in death.

They did not speak to her either, they remained seated or standing where they were, they did look at her. Sjeba came to her, stood very close, almost touching.

Felicia caught both her hands for one moment and then

with the greatest effort she controlled herself, 'you must see to it that there's enough coffee.' She loosened one hand and detached the key ring from her belt under her jacket and gave it to Sjeba, 'and arak,' she said, 'and cakes; cook all the necessary dishes, let the other women help you so that there's enough; it is still a long night. I'll be inside.' She turned and left the kitchen.

She herself took her little rattan chair to the room of her son and sat next to his bed as if he were lying in it. Some-one had made the bed with a clean sheet and clean pillow-cases; the mosquito curtains had been lifted back and hung over the silver hooks.

Outside it was dark.

The night light with the glass screen and the three pink girls was standing there but she didn't light it—it was not dark in the room; in the side gallery the large hanging lamp burned and the double doors were open—the doors should stay open. The two windows behind the bed were open too.

From time to time someone entered for a moment, spoke a few words, or just stood silently near the bed.

In between Felicia thought of all the people who were not there, who were dead or not there—and then it was for a moment as if they were there, in the room with her and standing beside the bed, in turn—her grandmother, her parents.

Once during that night he was there too, her husband, the father of Himpies, whom he resembled and did not resemble. Felicia shook her head; 'it is such a pity that you could not wait then, that you have not seen him once,' she said. She said it softly, whispering almost, as if she wanted to console.

Bear: he was swearing so terribly and without stopping, about Himpies being—'Don't, Bear!'

Toinette should have been with her now, they together; the child could sleep in the guest room—but it was her own fault, she had not even been willing to be sad about her that night.

Late in the night a woman entered; Felicia looked up—when she stood near her the woman took both her hands in her own, pulled them up, held them like that—for a moment it gave Felicia a feeling of unspeakable relief—then laid the hands back in her lap, nothing else, and left. Felicia looked after her: who, who was she, was she the dancer in the Dance with the Shell?

The man with the blue hair came too—his son had been killed years before. Felicia stood up and made him sit in her chair. 'Sit down, Bappa,' she said, taking another chair, and they spoke a few words about his son and about her son. Then Felicia escorted him to the door, 'thank you for coming, Bappa,' she said; he was a very old man now and he no longer dyed his hair blue.

She thought: his son was killed—in action, as they call it; her son had been shot from an ambush—that was not the same. Her son was murdered, she now thought for the first time.

Domingoes seemed to be in the room—Sergeant Domingoes who was serving on Ceram. 'You took bad care of him,' she said bitterly.

They brought her coffee.

Others came.

A very young woman, herself expecting a baby, bent over her, stroked her hands, 'madam's little child,' she said.

After that Felicia sat with her eyes closed tightly.

A glass of arak brandy, 'come, drink it.' It was Sjeba—a plate with a cake.

Still others.

The three little girls in the pink dresses stood on the screen, two on the seesaw and one with hoop and stick; they were there but because the night light was not on they seemed faded and small and flat, as if already they no longer belonged there.

The night passed.

The sky turned gray, the inner bay under it an even lighter gray; the trees were standing soaked with dew and almost black. The small parade of women with Bibles and handkerchiefs did not come out from under the trees to the proas—for her son there were no proas.

Felicia rose from her chair, unhooked the mosquito curtains, pulled them across each other and tucked them in carefully under the mattress; then she left the room, closing the door behind her. In the side gallery the lamp was still burning.

· VI ·

SHE HEARD the details later. There had been a small patrol: her son, Domingoes, his men, a few convicts.

They had not made contact with the Mountain Alfuras

and were on their way back. They had come down through the steep mountain terrain and were catching their breath in a jungle clearing. Her son had been standing there bare-headed, his collar unbuttoned (she knew how he had stood, his head bent slightly backward), when from behind the trees an arrow had come, penetrating straight into his bare throat.

He had fallen on the ground, unconscious.

The others had not known how or what, was it a poisoned arrow? an arrow with barbed hooks for manhunting? how to get it out? The old convict had come forward, he had said he knew—first make a stretcher from branches, as light as possible; they had put him on it, then the old man had taken out the arrow. Domingoes had wanted to bandage the wound, but the convict had said: hold it closed with your fingers.

They had carried the stretcher down in relays of four, taking turns at holding the wound closed. They had traveled as fast as they could, it had been very heavy going especially with the tending of the wound. In the end the old man had refused to be relieved from that job. One of them had run ahead to get the doctor: it had taken some time to find him.

Her son had not regained consciousness, his breathing had continued for a long time, weakly, but for a long time. But when they had finally arrived at the barracks he had bled to death; it was almost evening then.

Early the following morning they had buried him on a hill near the coast, with military honors.

The old convict had had an attack of hysterics, crying for forgiveness, saying that it was all his fault.

Later Domingoes came to visit Felicia.

She would rather not have seen him; in the very beginning she had found consolation in hearing people talk about her son or even being with someone who had known him, but now there was a resistance within her against it.

Yet she had not written Domingoes not to come.

He arrived late in the afternoon, they had tea together under the trees at the bay. He was a stocky man, with curly hair cut very short, in uniform, a nice face; she would not have recognized him.

They talked about little things, or she did—had the trip been good? was that expedition over now? what were his plans? how were his parents, still alive? his father dead— a pity . . .

He gave polite but very short answers.

She asked whether he still remembered her grandmother.

Yes, he still remembered madam's grandmother.

'Your father made beautiful things, I still have some— if you like I'll show you—do you want one?'

'Yes, ma'm,' he only said, and she did not know to what.

The name of her son or even of the boy Himpies was not mentioned between them. That was not proper, Himpies wouldn't approve of that.

Later, under the lamplight, they made a list together of the men who had been there; Felicia wanted to reward them for their efforts, give them something—especially the old convict.

'Shall I send in a petition for the reduction of his sentence?' she asked.

Domingoes looked at her, 'I don't know whether they

would do that,' he said, 'he has murdered twelve people, I think—that is quite a lot.'

To Domingoes she gave the gold watch and chain of her son, and his mother-of-pearl spoon—he asked for the spoon, 'to hold in my hand,' he said, 'the hand has a good memory.' She also gave him a golden fruit with an amber ball, although it wouldn't be of much use to him, she thought.

The remainder of the evening passed quickly; after supper Domingoes said that he wanted to visit some people in the village, and Sjeba and Henry. He could sleep with them.

'My son's friend sleeps in the guest room,' Felicia said shortly. She did not hear him come home.

The following morning Domingoes did not leave immediately. They walked together to all the old places. They stood in the green, quiet valley near the white shell from which the chicken drank—'the Leviathan who is too terrible,' Domingoes said.

'Did you know about that too?' Felicia asked.

Domingoes nodded, 'Mr. Himpies . . .' he said.

They climbed into the hills; it was as beautiful as always there.

They came back past the graves of the three girls, and halted a moment near the little gate.

'I've never seen them,' Domingoes said.

'No, neither have I,' said Felicia, 'none of us, I'm afraid.'

'Mr. Himpies did; he always said, the girls in the pink dresses, so he must have seen them.'

'I don't believe so,' Felicia answered, but she did not explain further.

'We didn't want to admit that we never saw them,' Domingoes added.

And Felicia said, 'Yes, that is true.'

They walked on through the wood, past the singing trees, past the arèn palms where the palm-wine mannikin was hung when they were tapped, past the stream; now they were speaking of my son, and Himpies, and Mr. Himpies, as if it were no longer a forbidden name.

Near the old bathing place they sat down on a bench.

Felicia was silent—she had wanted to ask, did you look at him when you were carrying him? did you call to him and say, oh soul of . . . ? enumerate his hundred things? as they always do here—he was still alive then—he was young, young people should live, perhaps you could have held him back then—but she did not say it.

They had come to speak again, she didn't know how, of the old convict. 'What kind of man is he?' Felicia asked. 'My son wrote me about him, do you think he is bad?'

Domingoes said, 'Oh, madam asks that because he has killed all those—but that was unintentional.'

'Does he ever talk about it?'

'Yes.'

'Is he sorry, do you think?'

'I don't think he is very sorry. There is one hope in him: to be free someday.'

'Does he long for his country?'

'Yes, he also longs for his country and he hopes that the woman who informed on him will still be alive, he says, for then he will—' Domingoes made a gesture of strangling, one of his hands high up around his own neck.

Felicia saw it: a strong brown hand, a good hand, around

a straight strong neck; at the same moment she felt an
ice-cold shiver in the back of her head—an old crooked
skinny hand like a claw on a young white throat, so vul-
nerable, and everything scarlet with blood. She sat straight,
bent her shoulders back as in defense, 'has he—he did not
want to harm Himpies, are you certain of that?'

Domingoes immediately brought his hand down from
his neck, looked at her as if he did not understand; then
his face creased with laughter.

'He harm Mr. Himpies, is that what madam thought!
He was like an old hen with one little chicken left, fluttering and cackling over it; we . . . we people sometimes
had a hard time not laughing at him, Mr. Himpies sometimes got angry but then he had to laugh too. When the
arrow came he was laughing with us at the old man—'

When the arrow came—like that, quietly—it hardly
hurt.

Felicia was sitting next to Domingoes on the bench; she
liked the beach in front of the house better, she seldom
came here—yet it was very peaceful and green; the thin
jets of water from the open lion's mouth fell with a slight
splash into the cistern, the children's bath, where now only
birds came. And in her brusque way she suddenly asked—
if he wanted to leave the service, was tired of wandering
around and longed for his own place, as long as she was
at the Small Garden (as long as she lived she would be at
the Small Garden) she would help him settle there. He
did not have to worry too much about the 'how' of it—it
would be as if he were her adopted son, the adopted brother
of her son Himpies; he could marry, have a family.

He regarded her; his eyes were dark seen from so close,

a bit melancholy, very melancholy; and with equal abrupt-
ness he said, no, he did not want to settle; and when
Felicia insisted, 'why not? do you suddenly not like the
Small Garden any more?' he self-consciously recited the
lines from the psalm, the lines about: who go down to the
sea in ships will see the works of the Lord and his wonders
in the deep—he said it in Malayan, the Malayan of the
Bible which is different from the spoken language. She
had learned the psalms when she was a child from her
nurse Susanna, especially the hundred-and-fourth one, she
had forgotten most of it, remembered only a few words,
lakh-lakh the stork, and Hua which means the Lord. It
took her a moment to understand what he had said.

'Are you going to be a sailor?' she then asked.

He laughed, 'no, not a sailor!' he said, 'but life can be
like sailing on a ship, madam.'

Later Felicia took him to the proa and watched it cross
the inner bay; of course the bell had not been rung!—
such a slackness in everything of late—and there went the
Sergeant Domingoes who would rather be a penniless
wandering soldier than settle at the Small Garden. And
her son had been murdered by a Mountain Alfura—her
son should not have been murdered.

· THREE ·

AT THE OUTER BAY

THE COMMISSIONER

THE OTHER haunted garden on the island was at the outer bay. It was a great deal smaller than the Small Garden, it was actually not very much larger than an ordinary garden such as one finds with a house. It was near the town and the highway. On one side of it was the outer bay, on the other three an impenetrable hedge of high thorny bamboos, with a huge wrought-iron entrance gate.

From the house the ground fell steeply to the beach.

Only one of the rooms of the house dated from the old

days and had old-fashioned brick walls, as thick as a man is high, with tall windows and deep sashes, and a black-and-white marble floor which showed some cracks, all of it rather worn and faded. Yet this must have once been the 'Sunday room.'

The rest of the house had been built later: a closed gallery, more rooms—only the lower part of the walls brick, the rest planks chalked white.

In front of the house was a verandah, painted green, with some rickety steps leading down to the garden and the short wide lane of plane trees which descended straight to the beach. A small open beach; to the left and the right more plane trees, in the center a ramshackle wooden quay. At the end of the quay stood a solid pole, made of iron-wood, too high to have been meant for mooring only. It might once have been a lantern post with an oil lamp at the top—a reassuring little light over the outer bay—now it certainly was not.

The quay extended quite far out into the bay; when the tide was in, the water was deep there and a large proa could moor. There was a strong current.

But the Garden was deserted. The old house stood empty and locked; around the bars of the gate hung a chain with a padlock, and thorny branches had been pulled through them. None of these precautions was necessary, no one would think of entering the Garden; no proa would moor at the quay. Oh no!

Who would want to meet the commissioner who walked there, day and night, through the house, through the Garden, and at times stood on the quay—with his back turned toward the bay?

He had once been a commissioner, administrator of one of the very small islands near Dobo, where the pearl fishers are. He was supposed to have been very rich, but he had a bad name. Had he swindled, had he blackmailed, had he been a usurer? Nobody knew exactly.

The first time he came alone. He bought the Garden at the outer bay and had the old house renovated: all the doors and blinds were fixed, and especially all the locks. He had bars put in front of all the windows except those in the 'Sunday room'—did he not want to spoil that room? It had heavy blinds anyway. He also had a lock and chain put on the gate.

Having seen to all that, he went back to Dobo for his possessions: furniture, old china, the women, money, and the pearls.

When his boat docked at the island, the commissioner had everything taken to the house immediately. The coolies who carried the heavy furniture wrapped in mats, the crates and the trunks, didn't have to help unpack, they could leave right away. Thus they had not been able to see a thing, only that there were four women: three old and ugly ones and one young slender one, but she had a dark veil around her face.

The gate was locked behind the coolies; and after that no one was ever allowed into the Garden. And no one of its inhabitants ever went into town or even outside the gate.

No one except the old woman who did the errands— she carried everything herself, paid cash, and never talked. When she ordered heavy things such as cans of kerosene or sacks of charcoal, they had to be delivered at the gate at a certain time and the three old women dragged them into the house themselves.

And yet it was told in the town—by whom?—who lived in the house, how the rooms looked inside, and what went on there.

In the Sunday room stood carved black furniture dating from the rule of the Portuguese. A bench, a bench so wide and long that a man could sleep on it, two chairs with low arm rests, a table, a chest. A black chest with sculptured garlands and silver locks; when it was opened a little bell sounded: ping-ping.

And on the black-and-white marble floor stood old earthenware jugs, the kind the Chinese once used on their junks to hold salt and dried fish and such: some brown ones, and a very rare green one with lion heads, the mouths gaping and rattan rope run through them as it should be.

It was also told what pearls the commissioner owned:

A string of eighty white pearls.

A large pear-shaped one, on a chain; the pearl was neither black nor white but steel-colored, with a faint hue of mother-of-pearl—a solitaire.

And then two earrings, two round pink pearls, exactly alike and without blemish, pearl twins.

The three old women, the witches, did the work and had to guard the young woman.

The young woman was the mistress of the commissioner. She was a beauty, she might even have been Arabic (the most beautiful women in the world are from Araby) and wore a green and red iridescent silk sarong, and a dark-green brocade jacket stiff with gold embroidery; she would use kohl to make tired blue shadows around her eyes, she would have a delicate bent nose, just a bit too small, and a mouth like a red flower, a bit too big.

And her skin would be dark, a warm dull very deep dark.

When she was wearing the pearls, never all of them at once, perhaps the white string around her neck, or the gray shiny pearl on her forehead, hanging between the two black arches of her eyebrows—what could be more beautiful?

She seldom went outdoors—she usually stayed in the Sunday room—but when the moon was shining, when it was high tide, the two lovers sat together on the quay over the water: the woman on the steps at the end of it, bent over and holding the pearls down in the water, and then up in the moonlight: sea water and moonlight are good for pearls—and the man looked at her . . .

Thus it was told—by whom? by whom?

And early one morning the commissioner was found at the outer bay, drowned, washed ashore not far from the Garden.

He was dressed in white cotton pajamas, sandals on his feet.

The commissioner had drowned!

How did he drown? drowned—oh no, murdered! of course he was murdered, because of the pearls!

Policemen came to the house; they had to break the lock on the gate. The house was locked up too, they walked around it and knocked and called 'open up! open up immediately!' The women came to the barred window and said that they couldn't open since they had no keys— but why, what had happened?

When they heard that the commissioner was drowned they raised their arms toward heaven and cried, 'Allah, have mercy on us! Allah, have mercy on us!'

Another lock was forced and the women were let out and taken to the town. A policeman and a police officer remained behind and searched the whole house.

Every chest, every drawer was locked: everything had to be opened with pass keys. When they opened the ebony chest it made a soft ping-ping, and in a drawer, itself locked, they found the pearls; and they were as it had been told—by whom?—a white string, a gray solitaire, and two pink ones.

They also found a lot of money and papers. Most of the commissioner's capital was still in Dobo, lent at a usurious rate and managed by a Chinese. The papers showed that.

The four women were kept in the town and cross-examined. The young woman was no Arab, she was a half-caste Chinese. She was not very beautiful—but very slim and pale. A rather shy, pale young woman.

She came from a shopkeeper's family on Dobo; her father was a Chinese, her mother a Papuan from the coast, where there is much mixed blood. The three old women were aunts on her mother's side.

She had been really and legally married to the commissioner, and she would inherit everything since there were no children.

At first the women barely answered the questions put to them, watchfully, suspiciously: a hesitant yes, or no, or perhaps, I don't know—they didn't know much.

'Who was this commissioner?'

'I don't know.'

'Where is he from?'

'I don't know.'

'Did you know him long before your marriage?'

'No, not long.'

'Where did he earn all that money?'

'I don't know.'

'Where did he acquire those antiques?'

'I don't know.'

'And the pearls?'

'I don't know either.'

'Did you like them? Did you wear them often?'

Then the young woman suddenly began to stutter, and blushed with fright.

'Me, wear the pearls! no, never! I've never seen them.'

'You've never seen them?'

'No.'

'Oh, come on now!'

'No, really not.'

'But pearls must be worn, mustn't they?'

'I don't know, they say so—'

All four of them called him 'the commissioner,' the young woman as well.

'The commissioner often brought a bucketful of sea water to the house, to bathe the pearls in. Sea water is good for pearls, but I've never seen them.'

'Well, in that case how do you know he bathed them?'

'I don't, I thought he did, perhaps.'

'Where did he keep the pearls?'

'They were locked away in a drawer of the black chest.'

'Did he take them out often?'

'Yes.'

'Were you there when he did?'

'No.'

'Then how do you know?'

'When the commissioner opened the black chest there was a little bell.'

'But how do you know he took the pearls out?'

'I don't—I thought, perhaps?'

Slowly they began to talk more freely, and all four of them said more or less the same thing: everything was under lock and key and the commissioner had the keys, of the drawers, the chests, the rooms—a fat bunch on a key ring. They were not allowed to see anything.

He was always walking about and watching. When evening fell it was worst: he went once to see whether the gate was properly closed, and then later once more, and whether there were no holes in the thorny hedge, he inspected the bushes, went two or three times around the house, checked every room, especially the Sunday room, and locked all the doors again. Locked the four women up in the house. Before it was dark he walked to the quay—from there he had a good view of the house, up the lane —and stood with his back turned toward the bay, and watched until it became too dark. Only then did he go in. Sometimes he went on walking around the house after dark, even when it rained.

'Why did he do that, was he afraid of thieves?'

'Yes, no, I don't know.'

And then the four women, each in her turn, became shy and shifted in her chair and said with eyes turned downward, 'the comissioner was jealous, very jealous, of—of everything, but especially of the pearls, that's why he did that.'

'What else did he do? did he drink much?'

'No, not much.'

'Was he never very drunk?'

'No, he couldn't, he had to watch.'

'Did he ever maltreat you?'

'No—'

'Were you afraid of him?'

Again they hesitated, the young woman, the three old women, and then said softly and ashamedly, 'yes, perhaps—'

It all made a good impression; they did not contradict one another and seemed all four rather timid frightened women who would do no harm.

'Tell us exactly what you did that day.'

And they related what they had done—what they always did, every day. The three old women worked: one had been to town for the marketing, one had cleaned the house and after that started on the laundry, one had swept the garden. Then they had all together started on dinner. And the young woman had knitted, she was always knitting.

'Did she never go outside?'

'No, yes, at times.'

In the afternoon when the work was done, when the sun had lost some of its strength, they might go down to the beach to get some air, all four of them.

'Would the commissioner go too?"

'Yes, we were never allowed out of the house alone.'

'Had you been on the beach that day?'

'No, yes, that day too.'

'With the commissioner?'

'Yes, with the commissioner.'

'And did you then go back in, and he locked the doors?'

'Yes, certainly the commissioner locked the doors.'

'How was he dressed?'

'In a white pajama and sandals.'

'Did he often dress like that?'

'Yes, we never went out and we never had visitors either.'

'Weren't you worried when he didn't come back in the evening?'

'No, the commissioner often stayed outside.'

'Did he walk around the house?'

'Perhaps.'

'Then you didn't hear anything?'

'No.'

'Nor later in the night, calling, or something like that?'

'No.'

All four of them: their voices did sound hesitant but it fitted. And the autopsy did not show anything which contradicted their statements.

A man in his full strength, without any signs of violence on his body—the fishes had been eating away at him, and there was water in his lungs: just drowned.

The four women were questioned separately once again.

'Could the commissioner swim?'

'I don't know.'

'Did he never take a sea bath?'

'Yes, sometimes, but he did not go out far—there are sharks there.'

'Did you ever bathe in the sea?'

Here each of the women hesitated a second, it was hardly noticeable.

'No, or yes, once in a while, once or twice we bathed.'

'Together with the commissioner?'

'No, never together. When we bathed he stayed ashore and watched.'

'Did you bathe recently?'

'No—'

'Not on that day?'

'Oh no, not that day! Before, long before.'

'Do you think he could have committed suicide?'

The women looked frightened again and said, perhaps, but they did not think—

It all fitted, except that the keys had not been found— the heavy bunch of keys which they had mentioned— not on the drowned man, nor in the garden nor on the quay nor on the beach at low tide. Had he been holding them in his hand when he fell? Had they slipped out of his pocket when he drowned?

The women were astonished and uneasy.

'But we told you that the keys are lost!' the police officer said.

It was not clear to them, and that 'not clear' sounded even more uncertain than 'I don't know' and 'perhaps.'

They were dismissed.

They took a room in a small hotel in the Chinese quarter; they were not going to spend even one night in the house!

Once they had to go back for their clothes. They asked for a policeman to come along, they were too frightened, they said.

Later the money, the papers and the pearls were handed over to the young woman. She looked as if she didn't know quite what to do with them, and she hesitantly made a cross on the receipt; the three old women all made crosses too; and they signed another form, the young woman had asked for that herself, an authorization to sell everything in the house. She did not want to keep any of it. And the Garden and the house were going to be put up for sale too.

The furniture, the ebony chest with the silver locks, the old china were all sold by auction; no one wanted to buy the house, or even rent it!

And on the first packet boat the four women left for Dobo.

Early in the morning they went on board. The young woman was dressed in a red-and-blue sarong and white jacket with lace, and walked in velvet slippers. A dark gauze veil over her hair, which was pulled back in a tight knot, her face heavily powdered but not veiled. In one hand she carried a parasol of oiled paper—she wanted to keep her white complexion—and in the other her black satin pocketbook with fringe.

The pocketbook had two compartments with two silver rings which could be pushed out from the middle to close them. In one was her money and keys, a white handkerchief, a green bottle of cologne against seasickness and a roll of peppermints. In the other half the tickets, all the papers, and the pearls: the white string, the solitaire, and the pink twins in an old pill box filled with cotton wool.

She would not wear the pearls but she did wear her new gold jewelry, hairpins, English sovereigns for buttons on her jacket, rings on her fingers and heavy snake bracelets around her slender wrists. She liked gold much better than pearls, and she was rich now. One of the old women carried her gold and silver box—for betel leaves—and her small spittoon of silver.

The four women did not look so shy and downcast any more, they were excited about the voyage they were going to make and looked at everything, nudged one another, and laughed behind their hands.

Thus they left for Dobo and no one ever saw them again.

No, no, don't believe it! there's not a word of truth in it—it's all lies!

The commissioner was murdered, murdered by his wife and the three old witches.

That afternoon when they were walking on the beach together and paddling in the sea, just paddling, and he was standing ashore watching, she called him, she had walked too far into the sea—it was high tide—her sarong had got all wet, and suddenly she had stepped on something sharp, or a fish had stung her!

'Oh, oh, help me!'

She called him—she had hurt herself so terribly, her foot bled so—she called loudly over the wind and the waves, and in her fright she even went in farther and almost fell.

The man ran out to her as he was, in his sandals, very startled, and when he was near her and bent over to look at her foot she clung to him, leaning as far as possible over his back, and screamed and screamed.

The wind and the water rushed so loudly in his ears, and her sharp screaming voice, so that he became dizzy and lost his balance for a moment and fell. She fell with him, on top of him. Behind her the three old women were waiting and the four of them held him under water—not even so very long—pushed him toward the quay, the deep place where the current was strong.

Then all four went to change, rinsed their wet clothes in fresh water, and locked themselves up in the house. They had taken his key ring and buried it in the garden; the one key with which they had locked themselves up they hid in the house, under the floor.

No, no! don't believe that, it isn't true, it can't be true! He was a strong man, how could four women—

Old women can be tough and strong, perhaps they had given him something to drink beforehand to make him drowsy and dizzy, every bibi has potions like that for sale.

Perhaps they had not even planned it beforehand, but when it all went so easily—

Why had they done it, for the pearls?

Perhaps.

Or perhaps because they were afraid of him?

Nobody knows.

But the commissioner has come back to the Garden— that is certain, everybody knows that.

And now everything in the small garden at the outer bay, the leaves of the spice trees, the cool wind from the bay around the old house, the waves of the surf, are whispering—whispering—

Keep the house locked, close the doors and the blinds

and the windows. No one shall live there. Let it crumble away slowly.

Close the gate with lock and chain, no one shall enter the garden.

Leave the spice trees alone and let them blossom and bear fruit and strew their seeds on the ground; let the weeds grow and choke it all up again.

The clover blossoms roll away and wither, the nutmeg fruits ripen, the yellow-green skin bursts; the coral red mace loses its color and blows away on the wind, the gleaming black nuts fall on the hard dry earth.

No proa shall come from across the outer bay, moor at the quay, throw its rope around the old lantern post.

The quay will collapse, even the strong ironwood post will rot away in the salt water.

Leave the commissioner alone! Give him time to forget everything: the garden and the house, his ebony furniture and china, the green water jug, his money, his servants, his wife, and his pearls.

Let him forgive the four women if they have murdered him—he should know.

Give him time.

Then he will leave, for this is not his home. But he needs time—time.

This happened in the same year that Lieutenant Himpies was shot by a Mountain Alfura's arrow.

CONSTANCE AND
THE SAILOR

THE OLD TOWN HOUSE of the lady of the Small
Garden was rented at that time to a young Dutch official
and his family.

A couple with a two-year-old daughter who was named
Sophia Pia after her grandmother; the servants said Miss
Sophy, and so her name was Sophy.

There were six servants living in—besides a cook—all
related to each other.

Old Matthew was Number One. He should not have
been a house servant at all, but the head of a Christian
village on one of the other islands. He should have been a
rajah, as they called it, even if he would never have worn
a brocade caftan with mules and a turban with an aigrette;
even if he had dressed only in striped cotton trousers and
a jacket, and on Sundays for church black trousers and a
jacket with sleeves of gleaming bombazine, and bare feet
—just as now—he should still have been a rajah.

Since time immemorial two families had been fighting
each other on his island for the post of Rajah; every now
and again the fight became a matter of life and death, and
several times in succession Matthew's family had lost it.

He could talk about it quite resignedly: the other family
was large, with many young and strong men; his family
was smaller and most of them older or weaker. And the
young defeat the old, the strong the weak, the many the
few; that's the way it is and there is nothing wrong with it
—in the end the young are the old, the strong the weak,
and the many the few.

'But many that are first shall be last,' said Matthew.

Still, it had been too much for him to remain at home and watch all this passively; he had left his wife and young children there, and once or twice a year he visited them. He himself had gone to the town at the outer bay and stayed there: an elderly man with little education—what was left for him but to become a house servant?

Not that he had much liking for it; but he always brought some relatives along with him and cleverly distributed the work among them. He was such a respectable and wise old man that any house could count itself lucky where he was the number-one servant. Most of the work was done by Lea, sister of his wife, and her three children, and by a niece Pauline, the grown-up daughter of one of his brothers.

Mama Lea was an enormous female, very dark and ugly, with a laughing mouth full of large snowy white teeth. No one understood where her delicate little daughter Lisbeth came from. The child looked a bit like a Negro doll, with heavy black curls, deep eyes like raisins and shiny white teeth, but her skin was light, the color of coffee with a lot of cream. She was nine or ten years old but Mama Lea dressed her like a woman, and when Matthew told her that Lisbeth was now old enough to work she combed Lisbeth's short hair into a little high knot, and Lisbeth became the nursemaid of Miss Sophy.

Her 'work' was to sit with Sophy on a mat under a tree from after breakfast until it became too hot, and then again in the afternoon after her nap until the sun set. There were dolls to play with, a velvet dog, and a real bird: a tame cockatoo which the lady of the Small Garden had given as a present. Sophia said 'ka-ka-tua' to it; those were her first words.

Pauline did the sewing and the ironing, and repaired the laundry. Pauline was a mystery. She didn't resemble any of the others, she didn't seem to belong to them, and she kept at a distance. She obeyed Matthew—who wouldn't obey Matthew?—but nothing more than that. A young woman, not very tall, neatly dressed in somber colors which made her seem even darker than she was; there was something constrained about her, as if she were holding back a secret behind that dark and controlled face—she was very lonely.

Until the arrival of Constance.

The cook fell ill, and since Matthew wasn't able to find another relative for the job a cook was brought from the town: Constance. She was not of his family so she did not live in. She had her own home somewhere in the town, she had always lived there and was an independent woman, she looked down on the others, said they were from the jungle.

Her face was not beautiful; it had no clear lines, was round and full like a child's face; her glossy hair was almost smooth and she wore it combed back in a little knot low on her neck—but when Constance came from the market in her straight skirt and jacket, the old brown basket on top of a folded kerchief on her head, and walked under the high trees, down the lane to the house and up the stairs and through the gallery behind the green vines with their blue flowers, to her kitchen—then everyone stood still for a moment and looked after her.

She held her long legs almost straight, hardly used her

hips and knee joints; the muscles of the round smooth neck, the narrow straight back, the supple shoulders, all held her head with the heavy basket proudly up, moved the hanging arms rhythmically with her walk, never loose and dangling, slowly, as if her hands were heavy weights. That gave her gait something stately and languishing: the way someone personifying Harvest or Summer in a parade would walk. Instead of the old worn basket she could have been carrying a tray with golden pineapples or a brass water jug glittering in the sunlight.

Pauline adored Constance from the very first day. She followed her everywhere, did unpleasant jobs for her, and defended her in a voice trembling with indignation when anyone criticized her.

Constance had once been honestly married but no one knew where her husband had gone and she didn't know herself. She now had a lover, as was her right—only it was a different one every day. And if she didn't care much for her lovers, the lovers cared very much for her. They always wanted to fight one another or they waited for her in a secluded spot to speak to her just once more—the very last time—and threatened her with murder and suicide; and everyone suffered except Constance. For in her heart she cared for only one thing, and that was the rattan tug-of-war.

Once, by accident, the young official and his wife had seen her at it.

It had been late in the evening, on a little square in the heart of the town.

The moon was shining but the foliage of the high trees was so heavy that it closed off the clear sky of the night;

under it, in the dark and the dust, torches were burning with a flickering, reddish glare and there were many people.

A long heavy rattan rope of pieces knotted together was lying on the ground in the middle of the square, and at each end a group of men waited for the tug-of-war.

On one side the drum players were sitting with their instruments—large ones, small ones, and very light ones like tambourines. Some played with closed fists, others with the palms of their hands; a single one played his airily with the tips of his fingers.

But the drums were completely and faultlessly attuned to one another—their music never became an anarchy of sound but remained bound in the severe rhythm, an all-penetrating beat; sometimes the rhythm changed, that was all.

It urged the men on during their intense efforts to pull the rattan rope, it whipped up their strength and hammered the weariness out of their bodies.

Whenever a team had won the drums stopped abruptly and left the men, the victors too, completely exhausted. Some let themselves go and fell down where they stood, others sat listlessly on the ground.

Then the women had to come and sing until the men had recovered.

The women stood in rows, forming a square: five rows of five, for instance, or six rows of six—close together and dressed alike, each with a large white cloth folded flatly on her head.

They sang songs, several different ones, and then over and over the monotonous song of the rattan tug-of-war which changes into a love song; and they clapped their hands and took a few steps in the rhythm of the music— forward or backward—they hardly moved from their places.

The drums started again—softly . . .

The drum calls, from afar, from afar—that is what the song said. Softly, as an accompaniment to the singing only, lightly marking the beat.

But then—not suddenly—with careful fingers, hands, fists, the drums took over: their beat, their tempo, their rhythm!

The words of the song, the melody, were lost in the thumping.

The women continued to clap their hands in time with the drums, stepping forward and backward in their rhythm.

The young official and his wife discovered Constance only after a while: she was in the first row but it was hard to recognize her among all those women.

In the flickering light of the torches shining red and turbid through the smoke and the dust, her face seemed almost black. It was dripping with perspiration, gleaming as if oiled; she stared ahead with wide-open eyes, seeing nothing. And she looked exactly like the woman next to her, and the one next to that one.

They were no longer rows of singing, dancing, clapping women but a strange unwieldy thing, dark, huge, square, covered with white, carried on a stream rather than moving —carried forward, backward, on the rhythm of the drums —the way the drums wanted it.

'Had enough?' asked the young official. 'What a terribly boring affair, imagine the beautiful Constance enjoying that.'

His wife walked next to him. Was that what he thought?
—she couldn't understand. Boring? no—dark, threatening,
exciting, mixed with an age-old fear—but not boring!

Constance, with the many lovers she didn't care about—
Constance's real lover was a drum, not one drum, all drums,
the rhythm of them, and a more passionate, a more tender
lover she would probably never find.

The following day she was tired of course and had to
sleep late, she did not come to do the cooking—Pauline
would do it—she didn't even send a message. Later in the
day she showed herself, quietly and gracefully, gave Pauline
her slow little smile and ignored Matthew's mutterings.

But one day she made a slip. Until then her love ad-
ventures had been her own business, but now—! Her new
lover was a sailor, and a woman who is not so very young
any more, who has some money, 'one of the town,' cannot
mix with a sailor.

It was terrible!

He was not even a sailor in the Royal Navy, nor of the
packets—they always have a lot of money and stay only a
few days—he was from a government coast-guard vessel,
the worst of them all.

He was not 'one of ours' either, not even from any of
the islands—he was from Macassar, he might even not be
a Christian!

Matthew wore a face like a thundercloud, he didn't
speak to Constance any more and he forbade Mama Lea to
talk to her (and Mama Lea enjoyed talking so); Lisbeth's
little brothers ran behind Constance in the street and called
her names, and Lisbeth herself tried with great patience to
teach Sophy the 'song of the drunken sailor.'

Only Pauline remained faithful, but she was worried and kept saying, 'be careful, Constance, be careful, it'll bring trouble, you'll see!' as if she could foresee the future.

It began on an afternoon during the siesta hour: Pauline came rushing into the bedroom of the house without even knocking, came to a dead halt between the beds. Her head was huddled between her shoulders, she held her upper arms pressed against her body as if she were supporting it that way, her forearms straight in front of her; her hands were shaking violently.

Her mouth trembled so much that she could hardly speak, 'the sailor, the sailor from Macassar, he's come with a knife, he's murdering Constance!'

She was such a frightening figure, the way she stood there with shaking hands, that the young official jumped out of bed, grabbed Pauline by one arm and crying 'come on! where, where is he?' stumbled out of the house in his rumpled pajamas on his bare feet—he couldn't walk well on bare feet. His wife ran after him, in her dressing gown.

The bedroom opened on the back gallery, and behind it was the garden, sunny and empty under the trees—there was no one to be seen. Through a window Mama Lea and Lisbeth were peering out with large frightened eyes. The boys had hidden somewhere in the bushes at the back of the garden.

Why wasn't Matthew there?

The house stood close to the outbuildings; to the right, near the back gallery, was the kitchen on a small gallery with long vines. The wooden door to the kitchen was closed and in front of it stood a man. That must be the sailor!

He wasn't in uniform but in a long sarong, black jacket, a thin dark kerchief wound around his head.

Constance was nowhere to be seen, had she been able to escape in time?

The kitchen door was closed, there was a heavy wooden bar on the inside and there were wooden bars on the windows—she would be relatively safe in there.

The sailor stood with his face almost against the door, knocking on it with his left hand, softly but insistently, and in his right hand he held a short, wicked-looking knife with the point down.

'Hey there—you!—are you mad!' the young official called while he hobbled down the gallery with Pauline.

The sailor spun sharply around, he pressed his back against the closed door and stood bent forward, staring hard.

The official's wife knew what would happen now: first her husband, then Pauline, then she; then inside, little Sophy in her bed, then back, Constance in the kitchen; after that he would run out into the street and be caught. That was how it always happened, that's how it would be in the paper: 'Sailor runs amuck—kills one two three four five—four adults and a child.' The young official first!—her heart stopped beating.

Then she saw the face of the sailor. It wasn't a 'dark' face —a young face, full of suspicion, watchful but at the same time astonished, as if he were at a loss about something.

'Are you completely crazy, what do you want with that knife? Give it to me!'

The young official was now standing face to face with him and put out his hand.

The sailor eyed him for a second—the official was young too, a scrawny fellow, not very tall, in pajamas and with empty hands.

What was he going to do?

Without saying a word the sailor held the knife toward him, but just then Pauline jumped in between the two men like a cat, and before they knew what she was up to she had grabbed the knife and run away with it, holding it in both hands.

For a moment it seemed as if all would go awry.

A wave of darkness, of fury, swept over the face of the sailor: wide-open eyes stared out—even the whites of his eyes became dark. The official shouted furiously, 'Pauline, you fool, what are you doing! Give that knife back immediately!'

But she was standing at a distance, holding the knife against her; one of her hands was bleeding and she was ready to run on. The young official would never be able to catch her on his bare feet. He shrugged, 'idiotic woman,' he said, and turned again toward the sailor, who also seemed to have calmed down.

'How can you—' he started again, stopped, looked at the other man, and then they both began to grin.

'You're quite right, sir,' the sailor said, 'I beg your pardon,' and he scratched his head.

They now walked side by side toward the lane in front of the house.

The sailor stopped. 'A woman like that,' he said and pointed with his thumb at the kitchen, 'drives a man crazy, sir, really!' and he hit his own forehead several times with his hand, the long brown fingers bent far back.

'Well, leave her alone then,' the official advised him.

The sailor smiled again, 'you're right sir, I beg pardon.'

Then he came rigidly to attention in his sarong and jacket, saluted smartly with his hand straight and stiff beside his forehead, 'and all the best to you, sir!'

The official in his striped pajamas saluted back, he had served too once, 'the same to you!' he said—what else could he say?

And that was the end of that.

The sailor walked on, the young man turned back to the house, 'are you coming?' he asked his wife, but she remained where she was to see what would happen next.

For the sailor was standing still in the lane, at the other side, under the high trees, and Pauline was rattling at the kitchen door. After a while Constance opened it carefully, and when she saw that Pauline had the knife, she came out.

She was still pale but her color soon came back, and then she walked toward the lane in her stately gait, Pauline next to her with the knife. 'Constance,' Pauline whispered urgently, 'be careful, Constance!'

But Constance did not listen to her. She looked at the sailor across the lane and the sailor looked at her.

And since they were lovers, why didn't they make up, why didn't they leave together and let Pauline stand there alone with the knife? They could go walking along the blue outer bay, hand in hand, Constance holding a green palm leaf over her head against the sun, Constance and her sailor. But no, they just stood there and looked at each other.

The sailor was not very tall, dark, lightly built, supple

and yet strong—there was something open about him; space, sea with white-crested waves, and a high wind—a green depth of water with a silvery fish fleeting through; he could have been the fish!

And he was young.

Compared to him Constance's feet were too flatly on the ground now that she was standing still, and it was as if a stagnancy hung around her, of air under dense trees, smoke of the torches, dust, the sickly beating of drums.

She wasn't really young any more. And slowly, in her indifferent way, she began to bait the sailor:

'What did you think, coming like this in broad daylight —you thought to embarrass me, I guess! You sailor, you haven't been sober for a week. And with a knife—thought I'd be afraid, eh? Ha! Afraid of you? What kind of a man are you, anyway? You are no man at all!' Pauline was standing beside her holding the knife.

The sailor stood motionless, only his eyes moved from one to the other, from one to the other.

Then he made a loud clicking sound with his tongue and cried almost gaily, 'Sluts, that's what you are, both of you!' And without another word he turned around and began to walk leisurely down the sunny lane, not looking back once.

Constance made as to run after him, but Pauline took hold of her wrists, 'Constance, watch out, he'll kill you!'

Constance tried to pull herself loose but Pauline did not let go, and so she shrugged and let herself be dragged back into the garden.

When they saw the official's wife, Pauline immediately burst out, 'Madam has seen it herself, Constance can't go

home, as long as that sailor is in town she has to live here
—she can sleep in my room, I'll sleep somewhere else—
she can't go on the street, it's much too dangerous: the
sailor will kill her—surely Madam understands that!'

Constance looked as if they were talking about someone
else.

When the young wife said, hesitantly, that it was all
right, that she could stay for the time being, Constance
did not even listen.

'Show me the knife,' she said to Pauline.

She took it in her hand, looked it over carefully, showed
it to the official's wife too. It was a beautiful instrument,
of good steel, thin and ground very sharp, ending in a
point. The handle seemed a bit too heavy for the blade;
a black rattan fiber was wound around it very neatly, one
loop tight against the other, so as to make it lie firmly in
the hand.

Constance moved her finger along the blade and drew
in her breath, 'ai—how sharp,' she said and closed her eyes
for a moment.

When Pauline wanted to take back the knife Constance
gave her a surprised look, 'but it's my knife,' she said, and
when Pauline muttered something, 'did the sailor come
to murder you or me?'

Pauline replied at once, 'no, Constance, not me—you.'

Constance kept the knife.

And then everyone went back to rest.

Later that afternoon, at tea time, Matthew returned. He
had been to the barber and he had had a glass of palm
wine (it was on his breath). When he put down the tea
tray for the official he said without any introduction that

Constance couldn't stay. He would find another cook.

The young man immediately agreed, 'Matthew is right,' he said. 'This time it all came out well, next time we might have a murder on our hands—no thanks!'

His wife thought that was exaggerated.

'I promised that Constance could stay here as long as that sailor is in town.'

'Why was that necessary?' the official asked angrily.

But Matthew thought it was all right, 'that will be only a short time,' he said. 'In ten days his ship is going on an inspection cruise to New Guinea. That's far, and it will take a long time. Let her stay here for those days, and I'll look around for another cook in the meantime.'

And so Constance stayed with them for ten days.

She didn't have to do a thing: Pauline took everything off her hands, cooked, scoured pots and pans, swept the kitchen, ran to the market as early as possible in the morning.

In her large basket she had a small one in which she brought a daily treat for Constance, paid for with her own money if the market money wasn't sufficient: fresh fruit or candied (and that's very expensive), nuts, cookies, or a bunch of flowers knotted in a banana leaf. Material for a new jacket which she sewed hastily, hastily, on the machine, with a long row of tiny buttons and buttonholes on both sleeves, to make them fit tight around the forearms.

She went to Constance's house and got her clothes, washed and ironed and pleated them.

Every free moment she was sitting with her on a mat in the shadow of a tree or in the gallery in front of her room. She 'rubbed' Constance while she lay full length on the mat, especially the joints of the wrists and ankles because it's there that tiredness nestles, and also the back of the head at the hairline—that is where man's sorrows and worries hide themselves. Pauline could rub well, and she did it while singing in her deep voice all the songs, all the psalms she knew.

She stealthily picked the rare lemons with the bobbly spotted skins from the one little tree, let them simmer for hours on a small fire until they burst open; after a night's cooling in the dew the heavy jellylike liquid which smelled so heavenly was strained, and Pauline used it to wash Constance's hair. She rubbed it in, then rinsed the hair with cold rainwater, dried it, combed it, combed it, sang for her.

Constance didn't object.

The sailor wasn't mentioned any more, and no one had seen him again.

Ten days' vacation for Constance, for Pauline ten days of heaven on earth. Ten days is not very long.

There were three blasts of a ship's whistle over the outer bay, echoed by the hills. Matthew raised his hand.

'There he goes,' he said, 'to the wilderness.'

And so Constance left too. She didn't mind, she had her own house and furniture, she had some money too. She'd look around a bit, when she felt like it she'd take another job, but not quite yet. The moon was almost full —time for the rattan tug-of-war.

She looked well and rested, her clothes all laundered

and neatly ironed—she wore her new jacket with the sleeves tight around her wrists, her hair glossy and smelling of lemon, a flower behind her ear. So she left, stepping through the garden, straight, stately, moving her arms from the supple shoulders—slowly, as if her hands tired her.

A few days later she would be singing at the rattan tug, dripping with perspiration, unrecognizable, half fainting under the rhythm of the drums—Constance!

Pauline came along to help her move, she said; there wasn't much, Constance's old market basket, her clothes, and the knife of the sailor. Pauline wanted to carry everything for her.

Then there were three weeks of silence.

At times it was so still that the murmur of the outer bay could be heard in the garden. Everything was as before, Matthew respectable and wise and Number One and nothing else.

Mama Lea did all the work and still found time to go look at the children in the garden, wet Miss Sophy's light-brown forelock and brush it upward, and comb out Lisbeth's curly black hair and pull it back so tight that it made the child blink.

The children played for hours and hours in the garden with the red doll, and the tame bird sat next to them.

Pauline was sewing and mending again. Often she would be gone for a little while—always to Constance. Matthew didn't object, he had only forbidden her to go at night when the rattan tugs were on. When Matthew said 'forbid,' there was nothing to be done about it.

In the kitchen there was a new cook, a man, his name

was Jacob; he was even older than Matthew, a sour, un-social fellow with untidy gray hair; no one cared for him. He insisted on cooking over wood instead of charcoal, and the clouds of smoke rising from the kitchen were the only way of knowing whether he was there or not. He didn't cook very well and he couldn't be made to understand that some people don't like turtle eggs. The official's wife hated turtle eggs and she began to think of trying to get Constance back—first she would have to convince her husband and Matthew.

But after those three silent weeks Constance could no longer come back.

Matthew told them early in the morning when he brought them their coffee in the garden. Pauline was with him, her face swollen and wet with tears.

'Be quiet, Pauline! I have to tell the master and mistress. There's been an accident, sir,' Matthew said slowly and emphatically, 'Constance is dead—be quiet, Pauline! Last night she was at the rattan tug-of-war. It was late when she went home, and there was a man with her. The neighbors saw him, but they couldn't see who he was. At dawn when they went to the well they saw that her door was open, they thought there had been thieves and wanted to warn her so they knocked, but received no answer. Then they went in and found her—dead—and there was blood everywhere.'

'Was she murdered?' asked the official.

'Pauline! Yes, sir, stabbed to death.'

Then Pauline no longer let herself be silenced and she

repeated almost the same words she had said before, 'the sailor, the sailor from Macassar, with his knife!' But she said them in a different way, like a child that is almost choking in a vast sadness, her mouth drawn, her face flooded with tears. She was standing still, her hands clutched together.

The others regarded one another—the sailor, what about that sailor, oh yes, he was gone, he was gone to New Guinea, the sailor wasn't there at all.

Matthew said softly, as if he were addressing a child, 'Pauline, listen, I've told you already, Constance was killed—yes!—but not by the sailor, no, that would be impossible. Figure it out for yourself, his ship left three weeks ago, it is there, in New Guinea'—with a gesture toward the distance—'the sailor is on his ship, not here! How could he have murdered Constance?'

Pauline had stopped crying, sniffed loudly, 'yes!' she said, 'with his knife!'

Was she losing her mind?

'Give her some bromide,' the official told his wife, 'let Mama Lea stay with her today, and tonight a sleeping pill —isn't that the best thing, Matthew?'

'Yes,' said Matthew, that would be best, she had a sharp pain in her heart now, it would grow less after a while but she herself did not know that yet.

They were all sorry for Pauline and so Constance was not mentioned any more. But in town it was told how the police were searching everywhere for the man who had gone home with her that night. He had been a spectator at the rattan tug, he had been seen by many people who would be able to identify him.

And after a few days he was caught; he confessed quickly. He was a man of the island, of the town at the outer bay, and he was Constance's husband! Years ago he had left her, gone all the way to Java, because even then she had been unfaithful—but then he had had such a longing for his country that he had come back. He had seen her at the rattan tug, and afterward he had gone home with her.

Nothing would have happened if she had not baited him, if she hadn't 'humiliated' him; in the end she had told him that he'd better leave, why had he come anyway? She was sleepy after the rattan tug. And she had pointed at the knife which was lying on a bench, gleaming, 'do you see that sharp knife, that belongs to my lover, a sailor —they are always ready with a knife, sailors; you'd better watch out, he's coming later tonight,' and she had laughed and yawned loudly.

Suddenly everything had been black before his eyes, and when he had come to his senses she was lying on the floor in her own blood—the knife was covered with blood —he hadn't understood what had happened, he had been afraid, wiped off the knife and run away, had even forgotten to close the door; the knife he had hidden in a ditch, he'd show the police—that was all he could remember. But when they went to the place he had pointed out, they couldn't find the knife—the knife wasn't there.

The story ran all over the town at the outer bay and people wondered whether he would be hanged or not, since he had made a full confession so quickly. But why would he have lied about the knife? or had someone else taken it away?

One day when the young official happened to be sitting alone in his room reading, Pauline entered; she sat down on the floor in front of him—she never did that—and tried to put her arms around his knees like a supplicant.

'For heaven's sake, Pauline!' the young man said impatiently. 'Get up, please, what's the matter with you?'

She scrambled to her feet, stood bent over with folded hands, 'I ask you, sir! I ask you, won't you go to the police, to the judge, to—to everybody and tell them not to believe that man, he's wicked, he's lying on purpose, he didn't kill her! The sailor, you know, the sailor from Macassar, he's the one who killed her, with his knife. Won't you tell them that I—that Pauline—' she beat herself on the breast with a fist—'that Pauline can bear witness, she'll take an oath on it, an oath on the Book, and also on the Box!'

The Box is the alms box in the church for the poorest of the island.

'And also on the—' she hesitated, but then she said it all the same—'also on the . . . the Water.'

It was terrible that she had said those words aloud.

The Water, that is the water of leprosy, and to say that to a European who is not allowed to know—she looked around, afraid that Matthew might be near and have heard, and then folded her hands again, 'I ask you sir, I ask you—' as if she were begging.

At first the young man asked, 'were you there, Pauline, that you're so sure? How dare you make such a statement? Do you think that man has confessed and is risking his neck just for fun?'

But when she repeated, the sailor—the knife—with that

same dull certainty in her voice, he tried to quiet her: 'Perhaps you think that the sailor didn't go with his ship and is hiding somewhere? I'll tell you what I'll do, when the ship returns I'll talk to the captain and ask him about it.

'If he says no, the sailor was not on board, then I'll go to the police immediately and tell them!

'If he says yes, the sailor did come, then he's been in New Guinea and not here, then the sailor has not murdered Constance. Do you hear me, Pauline? Or don't you?'

'Yes,' Pauline said slowly and hesitantly, yes, she heard him.

And still later, eight weeks after sailing from the town, the white government steamer came back from its inspection cruise.

There were many ships in the outer bay: two from the Royal Navy, a freighter, a black collier—the town was suddenly full of life, with sailors everywhere.

That same day the official accosted the captain of the government steamer on the steps of the Club and asked him about the sailor; he felt foolish and regretted his promise to Pauline.

The captain knew at once whom he meant; he had only a small crew. That sailor, the Macassar—a fine sailor, by the way—yes of course he had been aboard, why wouldn't he have been?

The young official muttered something about one of his servants being a relative of the sailor, didn't try to explain further.

When he was home he called his wife and Matthew, and the three of them tried once more to make Pauline understand that the sailor could not have murdered Constance because he had been in New Guinea, and the captain of his ship had said so himself! The knife she had taken away from the sailor and given to Constance was no longer his knife, she knew that quite well.

'And that's the end of it,' Matthew said severely, 'remember that, Pauline.'

Pauline had listened calmly and when they had finished she asked, 'and the sailor is now back again, here?' and she pointed with her hand to the floor right in front of her.

When they said yes, she nodded with a smile and went back to her work without another word.

The following day she was restless, wandered through the house and the garden and the outbuildings, sat down at times on one of the many stone steps, stared ahead, got up again.

She went out to the children but did not play with them, did not sing for them as she used to do; she sat on the edge of their mat with her back toward them and smoothed the fine yellow sand with the edge of her hand —a small area—and made a drawing on it with one finger, looking around to see whether anyone was watching her, then she erased the drawing again, stood up, sat down somewhere else.

It became late, the sun lost its strength and the garden was still, waiting for the night.

The young wife drank her tea alone on the front gallery, for the official had gone to play tennis; Mama Lea was tucking in the mosquito curtains around the beds,

Jacob the cook had gone home, and Lisbeth was already carrying the toys in. Only Miss Sophy was left in the garden on her mat with the red doll and the tame bird, waiting for Lisbeth to take them in too, and a bit farther off Matthew was leaning against a tree and smoking a self-rolled cigarette.

Pauline had not seen Matthew.

She sat down again on the edge of the mat and started drawing in the sand with a branch. She did not look around, there was no one, only that silly little child; she was drawing with short quick strokes, then she put the branch down and studied her work with a weird intensity.

She had drawn the knife of the sailor, the thin pointed blade, the overheavy handle with the rattan fiber around it —after a while she began to mutter softly, her lips moving incessantly.

She was so engrossed that she did not see Miss Sophy stand up behind her and walk toward her, dragging the doll along—walk with her little bare feet through the drawing, erasing what was left of it with the long dress of the doll which dragged across the ground.

With a cry Pauline rose to her knees.

'Watch out, watch out, watch what you're doing!' she cried at first, and then wailed, 'see what you've done! my knife, my beautiful knife—oh, oh!'

Sophy had stopped to see what was the matter with Pauline, why she screamed so.

Flushed with anger, Pauline grabbed the child by the shoulders and shook her with all her might. 'See, see what you've done!' She shook her so hard that the head with the brown forelock tottered as if it were too big and heavy for the small neck, like the head of a baby, and the red doll which Sophy held fast flew from left to right with violent jerks.

'See what you've done!' She gave the child such a push that Sophy fell backward on the ground with a thud, her legs up in the air. The cockatoo screamed and fluttered its wings—and Pauline at once turned around on her knees, grabbed for the bird which scrambled backward, screeching and pecking at her hands—she crept over the mat to get hold of it.

Then Matthew was standing next to her; he bent over and took her hands, pulled her to her feet, he did not say anything but just looked at her—for a moment it seemed as if she were going to attack him too. Then he let go of her hands, 'go to your room, Pauline,' he said, 'and close the door.'

She left without a word.

The child was sitting upright again. First she opened her mouth wide to start crying, but then she changed her mind, pulled the red doll toward her, brushed the sand off its dress, looked tenderly into its black bead eyes and started telling it in her own language what she thought of Pauline. But when she saw Matthew nearby she let go of the doll, stretched her arms toward him and began to cry plaintively.

He took her with the doll in his arm, put the bird on his shoulder, and walked to the house, where he placed the child in her mother's lap.

'Miss Sophy fell,' he said.

The bird climbed down his arm and sat on the table next to the tea tray to wait for a piece of sugar.

Matthew remained standing there, and then he asked without any preliminary for a week's leave: he wanted to visit his island and tomorrow the mail proa was sailing. The young woman looked surprised for a moment, he had been home quite recently.

'And Pauline also asks leave to visit her island,' he said.

'But she never told me,' the young woman answered.

'No,' Matthew said.

The young woman with Sophy and the doll in her lap was thinking: the mail proa did a long stretch across open sea, that was always dangerous. 'Why don't you wait for the packet?' she asked.

Matthew looked at her. 'No,' he said, 'impossible, Madam, that would be too late.'

The child whimpered the whole evening, until she fell asleep.

Later that evening there was to be a party at the Club for all the ships' officers.

'I'd rather not go,' the young wife said, 'can't I stay home with Sophy? There's something the matter with her, I'm afraid to leave her alone.'

The official laughed at her: when they were out late Mama Lea and Lisbeth slept in the child's room, Pauline too sometimes, and Matthew and Lisbeth's two brothers slept in the back gallery.

'Aren't six people enough to take care of your daughter Sophy?' he asked. 'They can call us if there's something wrong.'

She hesitated. 'All right,' she said, 'I'll come—but Pauline mustn't stay with Sophy.' She didn't know why she said that, she had not seen what had happened in the garden.

When they came home from the party very late in the night, Matthew and the two boys were fast asleep in the back gallery. Old Matthew sat up on his mat with a shock, he looked weary and uneasy. 'I fell asleep,' he said, and rubbed his forehead.

'Is that bad, Matthew?' saked the young official, 'did you want to stay awake all night?'

'It would have been better for me to stay awake, sir,' he said.

From the bedroom Mama Lea emerged with Lisbeth, tottering with sleep, carrying their mats and pillows. 'Miss Sophy has been very good,' she said, 'she hasn't cried once.'

The young woman nodded, 'thank you Mama Lea for taking such good care of her, and you too, Lisbeth, to-morrow I'll have a treat for you and for Miss Sophy and for Kakka!'

The child Lisbeth suddenly started to laugh loudly, right in the middle of the night. The bird Kakka was perched in his bamboo cage, where he was locked up during the night to be safe from the cat. He opened a round black eye and looked curiously around to see who was laughing.

'Are you coming?' the official called.

The young woman had the feeling that they were all one large happy family: the three of them, and the six, and Kakka.

Only the door of Pauline's room remained closed, and the room was dark.

The following morning everyone got up later than usual.

The young official went to his work. It was the day for his weekly card game at the Club and he would not be home for lunch.

Matthew and Pauline stayed in their rooms and began packing, but the mail proa was leaving only at sunset. The crossing of the open sea was done at night when the current was more favorable.

Mama Lea cleaned the house.

The young wife had put a chair out in the garden and sat with the children.

When Jacob the cook came home from the market he brought some news; Matthew and Mama Lea were standing with him and shook their heads about something.

Later Mama Lea told the young woman, 'there's been a fight last night, sailors of course,' and shrugged her shoulders contemptuously.

They all had their afternoon siesta.

When the young woman was having her tea, her husband came home.

He looked hot and tired, he collapsed in a chair without greeting her, threw his white hat on another chair, pulled out a handkerchief and wiped his face, repeatedly, stared at the tea she had poured but did not touch it.

'I've been at the military hospital,' he then said gruffly, 'that's why I'm so late.'

'In the military hospital—what did you have to do there?'

'Attend an autopsy.'

'An autopsy—'

'Yes, yes, an autopsy, have you never heard of an autopsy?' His voice sounded as if he were furious with her—'that idiot of a doctor asked me to attend an autopsy, and so I did, I can heartily recommend it to everybody!'

'Was it dreadful?' she asked, frightened.

'What?' he said, 'what? An autopsy?'—he shrugged several times—'no, no, it isn't so bad,' his voice sounded less irritated now, 'the bad part of it is done by then, the bad part is when they change a living human being into a crumpled piece of trash fit for the dustbin.'

She looked at him, surprised, 'but, but—'

'Oh,' he said, immediately impatient again, 'of course you never know anything—there was one of those fights last night, in an alley near the harbor, a lot of wounded in the hospital, and this one dead.'

'Yes,' she said, 'Mama Lea mentioned it—were they sailors?'

'Yes of course they were sailors, what else? It's always the same, sailors from one ship and sailors from another ship, and afterward nobody knows what started it—it is always pitch-dark, there was a woman with them too, one of the wounded said, or women—perhaps it started over a woman. Police arrived too late of course, and then they insist on an autopsy to determine the cause of death! Why?—it won't lead to anything.'

His wife had the impression that he went on talking but was actually thinking of something else; suddenly he interrupted himself and asked: 'Do you know who it was?'

'Who?' she asked, 'who?' She was slow in understanding him, but she felt nervous herself.

'God have mercy on me!' he exclaimed, 'who? the man we're talking about, the dead man. Do you know who it was?'

'No, no, how should I know?'

'Well, it was Constance's sailor.'

'Constance's sailor?'

'Yes,' the official said, 'of that day!' He imitated Pauline with her trembling voice, 'the sailor, the sailor from Macassar, you know, with his knife—that one!'

His wife lifted her head and they regarded each other in silence.

After a while the young man started talking again, he talked while staring into space, and he was drumming with the fingers of one hand on the back of the other.

'At first I didn't realize, only later—his face wasn't badly hurt. I don't know whether you remember him from that afternoon. I do.

'He was—what should I say, beautiful, that's such a strange word for a man—he was a fine specimen! A good fellow too, I thought, how easily he could have killed me with his knife then—' he shrugged—'well, anyway, such a young and sound body, washed clean and tanned by the wind and the rain and the sea—and then somebody picks up a knife, and what do you think remains?

'All his blood run out of him, that bronze skin dirty yellow, a horrible waxy yellow, and all those yawning wounds with curled edges and the flesh popping out— oh!—' he shuddered—'such a waste!' he said bitterly.

Then the young woman asked him: 'Did they find the knife?'

'I guess so,' he said indifferently. 'How should I know? It might be lying on the bottom of the outer bay, ten fathoms of water over it, what does it matter?'

A little cough: Matthew and Pauline were standing in the front gallery. Both in black, in their Sunday clothes, Matthew in long trousers and a full-sleeved coat, Pauline in a pleated skirt, long jacket, black slippers with the toes pointing upward.

Matthew said they had come to say goodbye to the master and mistress.

When the official's wife looked at Pauline she started—it wasn't Pauline! Even in those somber clothes she seemed another person, someone younger, someone who had been relieved of all depression. It was not her face, nor her mouth, nor her forehead that had changed—no, the black eyes, they hid a deep secret joy about something.

'Well!' Pauline suddenly said, 'well!' and her voice was a young light voice.

'Be quiet, Pauline,' said Matthew, and he repeated her 'Well.' 'We have to go, it is late,' and his voice sounded dull and resigned after hers.

The two boys were waiting in the garden with the luggage. Matthew took Pauline by the hand and they went down the steps, but on the bottom one Pauline turned around and said before Matthew could stop her, 'Well, I'm going! And the sailor, the sailor from Macassar, he was the one who murdered Constance after all, with his knife!'

After that she quietly followed Matthew out.

The young official and his wife remained behind in the front gallery with the tea tray.

'Will Matthew be gone for long?' he asked.

'He said a week.'

'And Pauline?'

At first the young woman didn't answer.

'And Pauline?' he insisted.

'Pauline?' she repeated slowly and without looking at him, 'did you think Pauline would come back? No, I don't think Pauline will ever come back.'

The young man and the woman suddenly took each other's hands, and when a moment later the little procession of every afternoon passed them—Sophy in front with the red doll in her arms, Lisbeth behind her and the cockatoo bringing up the rear in little leaps—they looked at it as if they saw it for the first time in their lives. The young woman started to cry.

He gave her his handkerchief. 'But you mustn't cry,' he said.

THE PROFESSOR

· I ·

A BELL in the corridor, a head around the door, 'Suprapto is to come to the director's office!'

Radèn Mas Suprapto, bent over his slides, had been waiting for this and yet it sent a little shock through him. He stood up. All at once there was a buzz of voices from the other assistants in the large laboratory. 'Suprapto, you lucky fellow' . . . 'watch out for the head-hunters over there' . . . 'bring me a paradise bird when you come back . . .'

He nodded stiffly, without smiling—yes, yes—but his heart was beating so fast that a wave of heat rose through his body.

Finally, finally something good, for once it was he! A study tour through the Moluccas with the famous professor from Scotland: a scientific expedition to prepare a new standard work on the flora of those islands; Rumphius's books of herbs would be the basis for it. The professor spoke no Malayan—he did.

As he walked alone down the long corridor a little laugh appeared on his face, just for a second; he was the man, for once it was he!

There he went—not tall, almost too slender the way a very young man can be, although he wasn't a very young man any more—in Javanese dress, the finest batik, ocher yellow and dark brown, selected for him by his mother in Surakarta. A short white jacket with long sleeves; bare feet—indoors he always walked on bare feet.

He was a handsome man: a bent, almost Semitic nose, the hairs of his beard and mustache carefully plucked out, his hair hidden under a kerchief. The eyebrows, as thin as pencil lines, the black lashes were the only hair on the fine light-brown face.

His hands and especially his feet were small and strikingly beautiful.

Yet he was not feminine in his gracefulness, it was a tense refinement of centuries, beyond masculinity or femininity.

He knocked, waited, opened the door, closed it behind him, entered the room, made a bow (shoulders and body bending slightly with his head), straightened up again, looked—

And then his mood vanished.

Of course—what had he expected?

At a round table sat the director of the Government Agricultural Service with the professor. The professor sat with his face turned toward him.

There he is, your wonderful professor! Yes, yes, how do you like that, Radèn Mas Suprapto?

Tall, thin, with clumsy hands and feet, in an ill-fitting suit of silk shantung, not very clean, with perspiration stains under the arms, bulging pockets. He had reddish hair, in his right hand he held a large wet handkerchief with which he rubbed his head, making the hair stand up in tufts. Red bushy eyebrows above glasses with heavy double lenses, blue eyes without much expression.

A thick nose covered with freckles.

And over the mouth with its square tobacco-stained teeth a droopy reddish mustache was hanging—why such a mustache, who in all the world had such a mustache?

His skin was as white as a girl's, full of spots and freckles, and the heat bothered him so much that his face kept turning scarlet as if he were blushing.

When he saw the young Javanese he immediately stood up, moved his handkerchief over to his left hand and extended his large clammy right hand, 'Aha, my young mentor!' and laughed, a short cackling laugh.

The director stood up and presented them formally, 'this is Radèn Mas Suprapto, professor—Professor McNeill,

Suprapto.' He spoke very distinctly, as if the other two were both slightly deaf.

'Wait, wait a minute, I'll never be able to remember that! uh . . . uh . . . Radèn . . . uh . . . Mas—but sit down, my young friend, no?' he turned to the director, who was after all the host, blushed, wiped his forehead.

'Yes, won't you join us for a moment, Suprapto?' the director said quietly. Usually in his office he kept Suprapto standing.

The young Javanese sat down with a little bow of the head toward the director. His face was blank.

The professor had fallen back in his creaking rattan chair, put away his handkerchief and started to search in his bulging pockets until he had found a fat notebook with pieces of paper sticking out, photographs, a pencil, and a rubber band around it all.

'What, what was your name? I must make a note of it—Radèn? Mas, did you say? That's a title of nobility, isn't it? I'll put you under R.' He leafed through the book. 'Remind me, under R, and then Su— how was it?'

The Javanese did not answer.

'Su-prap-to,' the director said slowly.

Yes, yes, Suprapto the clerk, that's the way you can put it down . . .

There was a silence.

The professor made a note of something, closed the book again, put the rubber band around it, no, took it off again—'we'd better get down to business—oh, my memory, my memory! perhaps you'll write it down too, Radèn . . . uh . . . Today is the—I'm going back to Bandung later today, I want to leave from there a week

from now—does that suit you, uh . . . ' he glanced at
the notebook, seemed on the point of looking for the
name again under R, then decided against it. 'We are
sailing from Surabaya, I want to spend two or three weeks
on Java first, mid-Java, the Merapi, the Principalities,
they must be very worth while? What do you think
. . . uh . . . Radèn, my young friend?'

The director said a bit coolly, 'Radèn Mas Suprapto
is from mid-Java, professor, his whole family is from
Surakarta—his mother is the sister of the ruling prince,
isn't that so, Suprapto?'

He looked at Suprapto, who did not answer.

'Ah,' the professor said, beaming, 'but that's most for-
tunate! It will be a pleasure to visit your family, show them
the person to whom they are entrusting their son—or
rather, to be honest, the old man whom their son has
to take care of'—a wink, a laugh like a cackling hen.

The Javanese sat motionless; he wasn't there.

The low-ceilinged open hall with the marble floor, the
sculptured wooden beams resting on red and gold pillars,
the gilded sacred birds in the four corners, green shaded
coolness from the high trees all around—a visitor! His
family (not his parents, they had died young, he had
never known them)—the woman who was head of the
family, whom he called 'mother,' dark, fragile, brittle almost, and at the same time unbreakably proud and
haughty.

He saw her look at the professor.

He saw the professor the way she would see him.

He saw her bony dark hand in the large not quite dry
white hand.

He saw them sit around a marble table, his mother on the couch, slender in one of her most beautiful batiks, all her jewels; she would pretend not to understand a word, she would not say anything, smile absent-mindedly and politely, listen to everything.

When the professor left she would look after him, watch him descend the marble stairs too quickly, stumbling (he might even wave), walk under the banyan trees— and then she would frown, close her eyes for a moment, look at her husband and at him: they were pro-Western, pro-European, were they not?

Well, there they saw a European, a professor! Learned —the way she could say such a word—a professor is learned! the professor of Suprapto!

Impossible: he couldn't do it.

How to get out of it? Not say anything now—he had already thought of something: he would get ill, send a wire to Bandung at the last minute. Give up the trip? Why?—that wasn't necessary, only the mid-Java part; go on board at Surabaya.

He now took out a neat little notebook and a pencil, wrote down the dates carefully.

The other two started talking together, shop talk of course, the director quietly, the professor excited, with his uh's, his cackling laughs.

Suprapto stood up and coughed. 'I suppose I can go now?' he asked the director.

The professor got up too, shook hands cordially, 'it's been a great pleasure . . . uh . . . Radèn, young friend, believe me.'

The director also said in a friendly voice, 'You'll have

great help from Suprapto, he is very accurate, and he writes the best hand of all of us, his drawings are quite meritorious too.'

'Ah,' the professor said, looking with interest at the small brown hands, 'that is a great gift!' He spread his own clumsy hands, 'I've never been able to master that, I write like a blacksmith, like a real blacksmith, you'll suffer from it, young friend!'

The young Javanese thought, yes, yes, the clerk, a clerk can write neatly and draw neatly—he bowed again to the director, the professor, and left.

But he had hardly entered the corridor when the professor pulled open the door behind him and called him back: 'Eh, Radèn, young friend, you'll take all precautions, won't you—prophylactic quinine and smallpox inoculation?' He squeezed his eyes worriedly, 'really, don't forget! Imagine if you got smallpox, I'd never dare face your family again!' the cackling laugh.

'Goodbye, my young friend! When do we leave?' he brought his hand to his head, 'oh, but it is in our notebooks, you made a note of it too, didn't you?'

The young Javanese said slowly, 'Certainly, professor.' Those were the first words he spoke to him.

· II ·

RADÈN MAS SUPRAPTO went quickly down the pier of Surabaya under the broiling sun. He was in Javanese dress, as neat as always, but now with a khaki-colored jacket, brown sandals and over the kerchief around his head an inconspicuous hat of fine brown straw. Coolies came behind him carrying his suitcases, neat suitcases; a little boy held his briefcase and camera. He was smoking and in his hand he had a thin rattan cane.

The professor was leaning over the rail of the ship, pacing the deck. 'So there you are, finally! They have already blown the first whistle—we would have left, left without you . . . uh . . . Radèn—I forgot your name again, young friend!' He calmed down a little, 'but anyway, you're here, good, completely recovered, did you have malaria? Take it easy now,' and he walked busily ahead to show him his cabin.

Nothing about the professor had changed: it seemed as if he were still wearing the silk suit of two weeks ago and holding the same wet handkerchief in his hand; only now he was also wearing a topee of heavy cork, covered with khaki and lined in green. From the back of it a wide cloth hung halfway down his back. Over his glasses he had clipped two dark-green sunshades—why isn't he carrying a butterfly net and a vasculum? Suprapto wondered.

It didn't surprise him when later he saw such a net and such a box in the professor's cabin, and a large silken parasol with a green lining. The professor explained to him how practical and necessary it was; 'sunstroke is no joke, young friend. I know from experience.'

He also showed him a heavy old-fashioned gold watch which he always took along 'on expedition,' as he called it, his grandfather's watch. It had never failed him; it was wound with a little key and he could make it strike the hour with a gay little tinkle.

Then there were two cotton bags which fitted into his coat pockets: it was his habit to get a supply of small change, in new silver coins, in each country he visited, and he showed the coins to Suprapto proudly: 'for the children along the way, when they bring us plants and flowers, you'll see what fun they think it! I remember how my good mother always used to give me a polished coin for my weekly allowance—it wasn't the value, it was the gleam it had! When I finish this supply we'll have to polish more ourselves.'

Suprapto nodded silently—what kind of man was this? was he completely sane?—he looked around the cabin. On top of a cabinet there were two pictures in a double leather frame.

When the professor saw Suprapto looking at them he took the frame down and handed it to him, 'this is my wife,' he said, and to himself, 'Kitty—poor Kitty,' and then again, 'and my sister, my good sister Ursel' and laughed.

They were good, expensive portraits: one of a woman not young but youthful, sweet, blond, with round curls all about her face, large round eyes with silky lashes, a rounded turned-up nose—but the mouth was not round, it was a thin dissatisfied mouth. At her throat was a cloud of tulle.

Sister Ursel was the professor without the mustache, with a pince-nez instead of glasses, straight hair combed high, a blouse with a stand-up collar.

'My sister Ursel,' the professor said again, 'without her—my wife is so delicate, has such bad health; I would not have been able to leave her alone—without Ursel I could never travel.' He stopped, looked out through the porthole at the sky, 'never travel any more, young friend.'

Suprapto suddenly asked, 'how many children do you have, professor?'; he knew that question was supposed to be Oriental and might annoy a European.

The professor turned to him, his eyes wide open and very light blue, he wasn't annoyed. 'I,' he said, 'I mean my wife and I would have liked children, we love children, but with her bad health—it was unthinkable.' And he repeated, 'Ursel, if it weren't for Ursel I would never dare leave her alone.'

Suprapto shrugged his shoulders almost imperceptibly, he wanted to leave but now the professor held him back, 'and—and you, Radèn Mas, young friend, are you married? Do you have children, how many children?' he asked with the same emphasis, and chuckled.

Suprapto said no, he wasn't married, he had no children. 'That is a pity,' the professor answered, and he muttered something about the severe rules he had heard of, the caste rules for marriage which were still in force in Javanese noble families like Suprapto's. 'Well,' he said, 'everything has its pros and cons, young friend, don't forget! To preserve certain qualities, outward and inward ones, in a family—that isn't so crazy! Style, for instance. Let your mother choose a beautiful young woman for you, of the proper class of course, see that you have children!'

The professor grinned, he was hot, blushed, looked past the other through the porthole.

Later in his own cabin, the door locked, Suprapto took out his portrait—he also had a portrait, also of a woman.

It was a bad picture, made in a Chinese shop, in glossy

black and white; in the background a stone balustrade with artificial palms and a volcano with a plume of smoke rising; in the foreground a rattan table, a vase with a bunch of paper roses, and beside it, she was standing.

She wore a Javanese dress and over it the straight coat which looked like a coachman's cape, of velvet, it seemed, with heavy gold soutache. It was a long coat but the stiff batik showed underneath, with one corner sticking out sideways, which gave a dashing effect. She was wearing stockings and embroidered slippers—with one hand she leaned on the rattan table, with the other she held her parasol; the very delicate fingers were covered with jewels, one ring next to the other, she also wore two round diamond earrings, the coachman's cape was closed with a diamond pin, and on the small round hat the marabou feathers were held together with a complicated ornament of gold and precious stones.

The woman whom he called his mother.

Her name was under the portrait. She was of such high rank that she had a male title—tuan Ratu—that is, Sir Princess. 'In traveling costume,' the caption added.

She was neither young nor old in the picture.

Against that background, in all that gaudiness, that clumsy coat, and yet so graceful, so slender.

Suprapto looked at her, at what was behind her: the country—his country—mid-Java, the Principalities—one mountain, the volcano, was in the photograph, but there was another. A pair, cone-shaped, rising in pure unbroken lines, so hazy, golden-edged, upward from the immeasurably wide plain.

A hazy sky above.

The palace with nothing but straight definite lines.

In the heart of it the women's quarters, walled; court-yards with trees, walled; bathing places, walled; terraces with balustrades, a large square with majestic banyan trees, high sculptured gates—which could be locked.

The people, generation after generation of men and women, with their passions—but how controlled, bound to old, old rules, approaching the perfect, never changing.

His youth there: as long as he could remember, this immovability, as if everything stood still and was: forever. No one ever cried or laughed aloud, nothing burned up in joy or sorrow—cool and secluded from the burning sun outside.

Afterward he had gone among strangers, on Java, later in Holland, pulled in two directions. As a young student at Leyden among many, he had hoped—he had had a lot of friends, a girl friend, young, sweet; he had not taken law like the other young men from his family, but had quietly started on botany, his favorite study, without telling anyone.

Before the end of the first year the bank had sent him a letter from his mother's agent, telling him that his monthly allowance would have to be discontinued 'for lack of funds,' that he'd better come back. He could make a trip to Paris first, stay as long as he wished, his passage first-class would be paid for him.

When he returned everything was ready and waiting: a post at Court with his mother's brother, the ruling prince: well paid, good prospects; the beautiful young woman, of the proper class of course, had been selected for him.

He hadn't married the young woman, he hadn't wanted the post, he had not stayed. His mother had raised her

eyebrows—that was the influence of those Western ideas
—if that was how he wanted it—he would feel different
later.

To Batavia and then the clerk's job in the Government
Agricultural Service—and now he was the assistant of the
famous professor, on his way to the Moluccas!

What good would that do?

When he looked at the portrait he knew that one day
he would go back, he knew that she—Sir Princess, in
traveling costume, and all that was behind her, plain,
mountains, sky, palace, the beautiful young woman of
the proper class—were his background, the basis of his
life, were himself.

But not yet.

Now he was still on a voyage, at sea, with his crazy
professor, going somewhere.

He took the portrait, folded it in the silk handkerchief
to put it back between his clothes, and then he thought
something he had never thought before.

He thought, when he was still young, in Leyden, when
there was still time, if she had then pulled one ring from
her slim fingers, or taken one clip from her ears, or the
jeweled pin from her coat, or the gold and diamond brooch
from her hat with the marabou feathers—but she hadn't,
the Sir Princess in traveling costume.

· III ·

THERE WERE so few passengers aboard that the professor was offered an extra cabin for all his papers and books.
He had brought crates full of books: not only books on

botany and Rumphius's *Book of Herbs* in twelve volumes with all the commentaries and appendixes, but also history, geography, ethnology, descriptions of old voyages, and last but not least, Rumphius's *Book of Curiosities.*

Sometimes while reading it the professor would call Suprapto in, 'listen to this, young friend!' and grin.

All the superstitions of Rumphius, about shells and coral, crabs with odd names, magical stones, all sorts of crazy stories . . .

And their conversations: fragments, snatches of conversation . . .

The professor and Suprapto on deck, on a bench against the rail—the sea of Banda as wild as it can be, a heavy, clouded sky, broilingly hot, the sea grayish and covered with whitecaps, the ship rolling—they were just on the edge of seasickness.

'Look at that boiling pot!' the professor said, and he grew a bit pale, and then he suddenly told Suprapto how a Scotswoman, long ago, had predicted a 'sailor's grave' for him. 'The odd thing is that there's something wrong in her story; a real sailor's grave, she said, body rolled in something, a weight at your feet and in deep water—but at the same time near a coast, a beautiful green coast. Of course I could get sick and die aboard a ship, but when you're so close to land I've always heard that they wait to bury people ashore. Her story made a tremendous impression on me, and—let me confess something . . . uh . . . Radèn, young friend,' he whispered, 'I am afraid of the sea.' And then the professor became very seasick.

'Why did you never finish your studies, young friend?'

'There was no more money,' Suprapto answered stiffly.

'No money, oh come now, and you from a family of princes with all its treasures!' the professor cackled, 'and money, oh there's always money. Has no one ever tried to get you a scholarship? but that should still be possible.' He fished out his notebook, took off the rubber band, a pencil—'just do your best for me these months, and I'll write you a beautiful reference and I'll push the director of the Agricultural Service a bit, and at home, I mean at my home, I'll figure out something—I'll ask my sister Ursel, she has a way with everything, with her everything is possible! She always has money too, she's constantly receiving inheritances.' He grinned gaily. 'Not me! I can't handle money . . . uh . . . young friend, I—' he made a note—'I'll write Ursel immediately.'

Suprapto's face reddened. 'That is very kind of you, professor,' he said, 'but don't bother. I couldn't accept that, I wouldn't want to—it is too late now.'

'Come on, Radèn, my young friend,' said the professor, 'too late? That terrible expression! Give it another thought —' he wanted to say more but only slipped the rubber band around his notebook and slowly put it back in his pocket.

He's glad that's the end of it, Suprapto thought.

One of the letters the professor wrote that night was to Miss Ursel McNeill.

A story of the Moluccas Suprapto had to hear the professor tell.

A young prince from Tuban on Java pours water over his father's hands during a ritual washing, he drops the basin, is slapped by the old man, insulted, and then has only one wish: to get away.

On a sandbank at the shore he draws a proa in the sand, with all the accessories a proa has: rudder, mast, sails, oars for a calm, rope, anchor stones in baskets, jugs of fresh water and food, fuel and a piece of flint, a brazier and a cooking pot, mats to sit and sleep upon, goods for barter, scales, money, and above all, arms. He thinks of everything—he is a clever young man, he forgets nothing, except one thing! He forgets the ballast.

Then, when the Lord Allah has answered his prayer and made his drawing into reality (and his brother and sister and his old nurse who want to come along have gone on board) the proa floats too high on the waves.

Ballast is needed! What kind of ballast?

There is nothing available but the earth of their country; and they carry earth aboard and throw it in the hold; then they set sail without looking back.

They pass many islands, and at all of them they weigh the earth there against the earth they took with them— the two never have the same weight.

Until they come to the Moluccas, to that one island— there the earth weighs as much as the earth of their own country, and there they stay and found a small state, and the Javanese prince from Tuban is the first Rajah.

'Don't you ever write poetry, young friend? You could make a poem out of this, an epic, in hexameters, and what deep meaning it has!' The professor laughed his cackling laugh, he looked Suprapto in the face for a moment and then suddenly said very seriously, 'You too, didn't you? You too had to hold the water basin and you too dropped it, my poor young friend, that is always the beginning—'

For once Suprapto did not control himself. 'A water basin, what do you mean?' he said shortly, almost angrily. 'I've never in my life been made to hold a basin for anyone!'

The professor shook his head, 'but you have, young friend, you have. All of us, always, when we're young, have to hold something for those who are old, and we drop it and want to get away, and draw a ship in the sand to reach a new country, and we always forget the ballast—there is no ballast but the earth of the old country—and the new country's earth is always just as heavy as the old country's—and for that, then, we have left and crossed the seas and might even have drowned on the way, in deep water, or grown old and in our turn let someone hold a basin up for us—you too, you'll see, you too, Radèn Mas Suprapto,' the professor said slowly and clearly, 'just like that other prince.'

Suprapto did not answer; so the professor knew his name full well, all that 'uh'-ing and 'young friend' was only to humiliate him—and just what was he getting at?

The professor wasn't getting at anything; he only made the little gesture—head cocked, one shoulder high—of a man who regrets something but feels unable to do anything about it—is sorry, he sorry for me! Suprapto thought, he sorry for 'the other prince'! For after all he was a prince—and he thought of the portrait.

The professor who without batting an eyelid began to talk to him, an Oriental, about race prejudice.

'Yes, my young friend,' he said, 'it is one of those generally accepted conceptions, and yet it's a misconception—that only the white man has race prejudice. I've done some traveling—' his eyes lightened—'and looked around, and believe me, it's not a matter of East or West, white or colored. One can have it as much as the other.'

Suprapto sat still for a moment with his head bent forward: it was certainly true. He knew—he knew how his mother, when thinking or speaking of a white man, could turn pale with an almost physical aversion.

The professor said, 'Such a tight little fence around us: caste and class, race and place, a whole list. And some of it associated with old, deep things—so familiar and so secure around us—but we, we of the mind, we can do without; we don't always want to, but we can go stand in the cold and the wind and see for ourselves. Isn't that true, young friend? See for ourselves—if we want to,' he finished.

The days on board were almost over; they had touched Bali and Lombok, Macassar and Banda—Suprapto often worked in his own cabin, doing unnecessary writing, just to escape the other's company.

At times the professor would put his head around the door, 'take a break!' or 'are you sure you're feeling well?' and had he thought to take his quinine?

'May I see?' he once asked, picked up the paper and

held it in front of his face, looked hard with his myopic eyes—why?—it gave Suprapto the feeling that his writing was hard to decipher; couldn't he even let him have the 'neat hand'?

The professor read all he had done, put it down, raised his red eyebrows and studied him attentively. 'No, my young friend, no!' he said, 'you're wasting your time with this,' and then without transition, leaning against the bunk, he delivered a short lecture on the subject Suprapto had been toying with.

He talked for a quarter of an hour without stopping, stuttered at times, cackled, winked—but the young Javanese sat motionless, fascinated; he was sitting in a room somewhere in a large university with many 'young men of the mind' (that's what the professor himself had said —we are of the mind). There was a deep silence, for here was the master speaking and they, they were the pupils and wanted to be; he too.

For the first time Suprapto did not think, the clerk, the secretary, nor: the prince, but the pupil—pupil was a good word, it didn't leave a bitter taste on the tongue.

The last evening aboard, in the extra cabin, in easy chairs; the professor kept ringing for iced water—it was terribly hot—then he switched to Scotch whisky, 'and you, young friend? oh no, of course not, you're not allowed to, a Mohammedan youth of good family!' and cackled loudly.

On his knees he was holding Rumphius's *Book of Curiosities,* he leafed through it, 'about jellyfish,' he said, taking the pipe out of his mouth and suddenly beginning to read, clearly and softly, like a woman almost:

' "Holothuriae, the 'mizzen': they have many names, small galleon, Portuguese man-of-war, sea cucumber"— they have little sails, wide at the bottom, small at the top— listen to this! "The mizzen can lower or raise this little sail when it feels the wind and wants to sail. Under water a mass of streamers, four or five feet long, hang down from it; the color is a beautiful blue, through which however something green plays. The body is transparent, as if a crystal bottle had been filled with blue-green aqua fortis.

' "The sails are milk-white with an upper edge of purple or violet, beautiful to behold, as if the creature were a precious jewel."

'And this: "it is miraculous to see a whole fleet of them, a thousand little ships—all together!"—and when Rumphius dictated that, my young friend, he was blind, blind as a bat; his wife and daughter had been killed by a crumbling wall during an earthquake; all his work, a lifetime of work, all his drawings, were lost except a hundred pages—and after all that: "it is miraculous to see a whole fleet of them, a thousand little ships." Doesn't it make us, you and me, seem like ungrateful dogs?'

Suprapto stiffened; the professor knew, he should know, he had just said so, that he was a Mohammedan—and then to compare him to a dog! And always that *Book of Curiosities*—why didn't he stick to his plants? That was his commission, that was why the Service had put a clerk at his disposal—not to be compared to a dog and read to about the 'little mizzen.'

He felt deeply hurt by that word 'dog,' and—strangely!
—also by the 'little mizzen' of Mr. Rumphius.

The island in the Moluccas, the island of the Small
Garden, the town at the outer bay, the hotel on the Castle
Square.

The professor gave Suprapto the nicer and larger of
the two rooms: there had to be space in it for extra
tables, for now the work on the herbs book began in
earnest: twelve volumes, trees, plants, flowers, prepare
slides, identify, make drawings.

The professor passed in and out, looked at what he
did, gave instructions, dictated.

On the days when they did not go into the country
they walked along the bay after tea 'to get acclimatized';
afterward the professor went down to the Club, sat on
the verandah or went inside for a game of cards. He had
a drink, sometimes one too many, laughed at all the
stories, told stories himself, stuttered, cackled, looked at
some officer's pretty wife and said Hebe, cup-bearer of the
gods.

The others laughed a bit at the old man and the Hebes
laughed too: not much, though, and not loudly.

In the beginning the professor had taken his Javanese
assistant along but after a few times Suprapto did not
want to go any more and looked for excuses; to be ridic-
ulous is humiliating for a man, an attack on his dignity—
if the other didn't realize that—anyway, he did not want
to enter the place any longer.

They met other people in the town at the outer bay; they met the lady of the Small Garden.

Suprapto thought her a little plump woman, a bit too forward—she invited them both to the Garden at the inner bay; she also had the books of Rumphius, she also liked to talk about Rumphius all the time, and she herself had once seen a 'little mizzen.'

And their expeditions: first, on the peninsula of the town itself; later they would have to go farther and proas would be needed. The professor didn't like proas.

They set out early, in the cool of the morning, always the same procession: the tall red-haired white man in a wrinkled suit, a topee with a fluttering tail of cloth, the large vasculum on a strap, walking under his big green-lined parasol; next to him the small slender Javanese, neat and correct, all brown and beige, with the gleam of really good batik work on his kerchief and sarong.

Everywhere they were besieged by children with flowers and plants torn from the hedges and ditches. The professor stood amidst them, had Suprapto hold his parasol, distributed coins (those first times he gave away pennies only), sometimes he brought out his watch and made it chime for them; he drew pictures in the sand, nodded and shook his head vehemently, laughed at them, patted them on the back. Suprapto did not have to say much. The more clever ones soon understood that they shouldn't pick the plants themselves but only point out where strange ones were growing, that the professor and his assistant wanted to dig them up themselves. After that, dimes and quarters were produced too, but the professor wasn't too liberal with his polished dimes and quarters.

Most of these trips Suprapto would forget, but one he would not.

It was one of the earliest: from the town at the outer bay to the farthest point of the peninsula where one of the three rajahs with Portuguese names lived, a helpful man and himself an amateur botanist.

A path along the outer bay with a surface of coral and shells which crunched under their feet, very dusty, open at first. In spite of hat and parasol the professor was suffering from the heat and whenever they passed some trees he paused, wiped his face, tried to fan himself with his handkerchief, looked up at the greenness and said, 'I like trees, I like shade, young friend.'

A long silent road of hours without people, without children.

Halfway there they came upon a steep stretch, where foothills of the mountains reached to the outer bay. There it was still untouched jungle; a little river rushed downward in a bed of red rock and loose stones. They had to cross a bridge, recently repaired with wood that was still green, under a roofing of newly cut palm leaves.

Across the bridge the mountain slope on their left was burned off, from the edge of the path to the top of the slope. Charred pieces of tree trunk lay between little plots of groundnuts and maize; there were some poor and shabby huts standing nearby. One of the huts was lower down than the others, almost at the road; it was better constructed and much larger.

Not a soul was in sight, neither in the field nor on the road, nor on the other side of the road where a short wide path led along the river to the beach.

Some ramshackle winged proas were lying there: large

ships, moored by long rattan cables tied around mountain stones.

The surf of the outer bay rolled in up to the roots of the trees, a cool breeze moved the foliage, some pieces of colored bunting bound to the masts fluttered soundlessly—nothing else moved, all was still.

Yet this was a settlement! Had they been seen, had the people fled from them into the wood? What kind of people? Suprapto understood, these weren't people from the island, they were Binongkos, 'the sea tramps,' many of whom came from the island Buton; they built those large seaworthy proas and wandered over the water in small groups, landed here or there, burned off the jungle, built some huts, raised a crop, caught fish from a bay, and vanished again, leaving nothing behind but the charred earth. They were a strange shy kind of people, speaking a language no one understood; and no one wanted to have anything to do with them.

When the professor and Suprapto had rested in the shade of the roofing and marched on, they passed the large hut and Suprapto saw that there were people there after all.

Against its outer wall, on a plank laid on two stones, some young men were sitting. They were in rags, almost naked, sitting motionless against the dark bamboo wall with which they did not contrast—they were so dark themselves, the small squat bodies, the immobile faces like brown clay, the black, stupid eyes staring ahead.

All four of them held machetes on their knees, which reflected the sunlight in sharp little sparks—these seemed to be the only part of them that was alive.

Suprapto felt a choking fear in his throat as he passed

them and his knees trembled, he clutched his little cane—
what was he doing with a little cane?—the professor
walked unconcerned at his side under the parasol.

They had passed—Suprapto had to look back, stealthily:
the men were sitting there as motionless as before but
all of them must have turned their heads, for the staring
black eyes had followed them, looked at their backs, their
unprotected backs—if the professor would only keep moving, if in the name of Allah he wouldn't take it into his head
to stand still.

The professor stood still, 'look there, young friend,'
he said.

Down the burned-off slope a child came running, jumping—it was a girl, a sad dirty creature, scarcely dressed
in a torn piece of cloth bound up like a sarong, her hair
knotted together with grass stalks. In both hands she
held a bunch of wild orchids with long, rudely broken-
off stems.

Was it because of the burned-off jungle, the ashes
perhaps, the sunlight? Nowhere ever bloomed such
orchids: clusters and clusters of enormous flowers, not
of one color only, lilac and pink and purple and yellow
and brown together; even the leaves of one flower were
sometimes of different colors, or striped or spotted. The
flowers bobbed up and down, and it seemed as if the
girl came running with a cluster of gaudy fluttering butterflies in her hands.

She stopped, stood immobile as a rock in front of the
professor, and breathlessly handed him the bouquet.

'Young friend, give me a hand!' The professor closed
his parasol and gave it to Suprapto, took the flowers from

the girl and looked at her, 'thank you, thank you, sweet girl!' he said slowly and clearly, as if she would understand that way, and to Suprapto, 'but look, look! If Kitty and Ursel could see this!'

He pulled his large botanical case forward, opened it, carefully put the flowers in—they filled it completely—closed it and pushed it back to his side. The girl watched every movement with big eyes.

Then the professor made her open one hand, produced a polished quarter and closed her fingers over it; then the other hand. 'You can't stand on one leg, girl,' he said and laughed. The child looked at him and laughed too, she held her fists stiffly closed around the coins. Suddenly a shock went through her—one of the four young men had called out to her, something short and threatening.

With feverish movements and as fast as lightning the girl brought her fists together and put the two coins in one hand, then grabbed them with the other, shouted something back—her face distorted with fury and fear—then put both quarters in her mouth to have her hands free, and clambered back up the hillside on hands and feet. She vanished into the wood like a little hunted animal.

Suprapto pushed the parasol into the professor's hand.

'Quick!' he said in a curt commanding voice, 'quick, you can't stand here, please walk on with me!' because in a brief glimpse he had seen how the four young men had come to their feet and were holding their machetes in their hands.

When they were out of sight, Suprapto said, 'This won't do, professor, you can't go into the jungle unarmed!'

The professor answered with his little jokes, 'can you see me with a pistol? they always go off by themselves!' and 'unarmed? I still have my sharp plant knife, young friend. And who would want to harm us? Oh, you mean those four obscure fellows on that bench' (so he had seen them after all), 'you think they—? But why would they?'

Suprapto said in an even voice, 'perhaps they like polished dimes and quarters too.'

'Do you really think so?' asked the professor, 'well, in that case they can have some on the way back, eh, young friend, a quarter each?'

They had not passed them on the way back, they had taken another road, a bypass through the mountains.

The professor was to mention the little mizzens once again. It happened during their afternoon stroll through the town, first around the Castle and then up a wooden staircase to the fortress; they sat on a bench on the earthen wall of the fort and watched the sun set in the outer bay.

Suprapto hadn't felt well the past days, he was withdrawn, more silent than ever. The professor seemed a little off-key too, restless, not making his usual jokes. He kept putting his hand to his head, complained about his memory—'do you think I'm coming down with malaria?' —and then Suprapto must describe the first symptoms to him; he would know.

Suprapto sat next to him on the bench—oh, that eternal bay, that green coast, that little surf, always the sun setting and rising once more, eternally the professor complaining about his imagined ailments—at times a large ship lay anchored in the bay, a man could stare at it and become melancholy—the eternal departing, the eternal saying goodbye . . .

'You know, I've been taking quinine for some time now,' the professor said, 'do you think that's it, or is it the heat, or is it my eyes after all?' He squinted behind his heavy glasses, 'but I don't only sleep badly, as soon as I lie down I get dizzy. When you had that attack of malaria before we went on this expedition, did you have dizzy spells when you lay down, and ringing in your ears?'

He did not talk on, nor did he wait for an answer.

Only after some time did he continue, but no longer in that plaintive, old-woman's voice—it was as if something in his being had shifted place, changed.

He spoke quietly, hardly addressing the other, no 'young friend,' no stuttering, no cackling. His eyes, wide open, light blue, stared—'and several times already, between waking and sleeping, I was on the sea, in the sea—I can't quite explain; there is a sea and I'm there, there is also a high shore with trees, and the wind blows, and then comes —you remember—' he smiled—'the fleet of a thousand little ships, all together, the "mizzens" with their sails of glass, of crystal, transparent, with violet edges, and large —you don't know how large!—and I'm there too, and then all those sails come from every side and go past me and behind and in front of me and through and over me.

'It does not hurt but there is an indescribable sound as from a harp string drawn too tight, only a thousand times louder—it is as if my eardrums will burst—'

He stopped, squinted, 'it is glorious,' he said then, and, turning to the other, went on in his normal voice, 'I wish you could see it. And you can believe me or not, young friend! It reconciles me with my sailor's grave, if it has to be that way.'

Suprapto did not answer. Why tell a thing like that? One shouldn't tell a thing like that—what was he supposed to say? He glanced at the professor, tried to see his eyes behind the glasses, the light-blue, somewhat empty eyes.

Was the professor turning blind? He had bad eyes, obviously; and day after day the glare, the sun on the waves of the bays, on the white surfaces of the roads? His dizzy spells? Ringing in the ears, sounds like a tight harp string? He had heard of that—but no, it wasn't acceptable, he didn't want it.

He thought, this man is too good to turn blind; and at the same time: if he goes blind, would I have to stay with him, like the son of Rumphius who stayed with his blind father and did everything for him, wrote everything down, drew it all anew? (he could write and draw well too)—no, he didn't want that, he didn't have to, they weren't father and son.

Between them was no bond, not a single one, neither a bond of love nor of hatred.

For he didn't hate the professor, why should he, what harm had the man done him? Oh, he knew—he felt it somewhere, not even consciously—how those awkward fingers were loosening up something in him, things which were too tight, too cold, which were destroying him: his youth, the fears and bitterness of a youth, his life, the world, a world filled with lovelessness—and taking the place of those were the professor's silly little things: his jokes and stories—beautiful flowers—look there, young friend! and 'we of the mind'—and shouldn't Ursel be able to get him a scholarship—'the other prince'—the quinine he pursued him with (why not castor oil!)—the good word 'pupil'—the crystal sails of the 'little mizzen' jellyfish—but he didn't want this!

He did not want a bond between them, not of one kind nor of the other—he did not want to stay with him.

That afternoon for the first time he gave the professor his hand to help him down the stairs of the fortress; later, walking beside him in the dusk on their way back to the hotel, Radèn Mas Suprapto took a firm decision: he was going to leave, he would not stay any longer—not even until the end of the expedition. He would write his director so that he could send another clerk; that would take some time. It would cost him his job, that couldn't be helped, he'd go back—oh well, back . . .

And why think that the professor was going blind? He might just be coming down with malaria, that's what he seemed to insist on himself anyway.

Not the professor but Suprapto was coming down with malaria; that same night after their walk, they had just entered the hotel, it began: he became nauseated, shook as if freezing, his teeth chattered. The professor was immediately with him, called the room boy, the manager. He held up Suprapto's head for him to vomit into a basin, made him rinse his mouth afterward; when he was undressed and in bed he put hot-water bottles against his body, covered him with a striped army blanket, put a wet compress on his head, took his temperature. Then he went to get the doctor from the Club. Suprapto vaguely remembered their voices: the professor terribly worried— was it malaria tropica? was it dangerous? The young man had recently had another attack, what should be done? The doctor, a bit ironical—it would probably be ordinary malaria, a good thing he had quinine, he'd come back tomorrow for a look—and also: the professor was supposed to visit the Rajah on the peninsula the next day— yes, he could certainly go! The patient would just stay in bed like a good boy and swallow his medicine. If the professor would come along with him, he'd give him the medicine. The professor told the room boy to stay in front of the door until he returned.

It was evening outside, in the room a wall lamp was burning. Suprapto was lying stiffly, flat on his back, his head on a pillow—the compress had fallen off, his body felt like a hard piece of wood that slowly began to burn with little dry flames from the feet up. At first it did not matter, especially after the shaking and the helpless shivering, but the higher the flames crept the hotter they became; at the same time a palpitating began everywhere in his head, behind his temples, in his neck—he had a terrible headache!—and behind his eyes pain and heat were radiating as if they would scorch his eyes. His lips burst and his tongue was too dry to wet them, the pillowcase became as hot as his head upon it.

They were on their way to the Rajah, walking on the

white road in the white sunlight, so sharp, so sharp, it made his eyes hurt so—he pressed them closed, turned his head to where the pillow was cool—under green trees, in the shade, and farther down the outer bay shimmered through the palms, deep, deep, an almost night blue, and the professor said, 'I like trees so.'

His head glowed so that the pillow was already no longer cool; he was too tired to turn it—the burned-off slope, the rough red earth radiated heat, the charred tree trunks smoldered with red flashes through the black, in front of the huts there were fires, red, and from the machetes of the four men in a row red sparks flew, all the time—any moment everything could burst into flame and burn down.

Suprapto tried his utmost to sit up straight; he had to get up, there was something wrong! He only moved his head to the other side of the pillow—cool!

They were standing on the covered bridge under the roof made of moist green palm leaves, the little river flowed by in its bed of stones, down to the beach where under the trees in the shade the proas were lying at anchor, proas to sail the seas in rain and wind, in pouring rain and storm, he tried to drink the pouring rain with his scorched mouth, and the storm wind.

When the pillow under his head was hot again they had to move on—past the small settlement, past the burned-off mountain slope, past the four men in a row. And again all was on fire, charred, black with red, and full of red sparks from the machetes.

Again Suprapto tried to get up—there was something wrong, he had to get up.

He didn't know how but he had turned the pillow—
cool, cool—they were under the trees, past the settlement
and past the four men with their knives. The girl came
running down the slope with the butterflies in her hands
—they were flowers, soft and wet with dew, lilac and
pink and purple and yellow and cool and cool and cool—
'look there, young friend!' the professor said.

And then everything turned black for Suprapto.

He was long and dangerously ill—it had been 'tropica'
after all. When the fever abated he was exhausted, very
weak; he did not seem to wonder why the professor
wasn't there, he didn't ask anything. The doctor had
given orders not to tell him about it yet.

The first time he consciously thought about the professor was one night. He woke up dripping with perspiration but didn't ring the bell to be helped; he got up alone,
dizzily clutching the edge of the round marble table—
the night lamp gave a dim light.

On the table stood a wooden box, of the kind that was
sold in the Chinese quarter—white wood with six long
thin dark-green bottles of cologne, wrapped in gray tissue
paper. The box was open, the cover was lying next to
it, one bottle had been opened and the cork loosely put
back on again. There was a note: 'You're to have
compresses, half water, half cologne—I've told the room
boy. Take good care of yourself, young friend, I'll be back
shortly!' And only an initial: McN.

A portrait was propped up against the box, the Sir
Princess in traveling costume. He picked it up.

How had the portrait got there? Had he himself left it

out on the table, folded in the handkerchief, before he fell ill? Had the professor found it and put it there?—then he had seen her, he had not wanted him to see her—would he have seen her as she was, had he seen what was behind her? How could he—had he seen—? He put the picture back against the box of cologne bottles, with the note, went to the basin, rubbed himself dry with a towel, had a drink of water, and crept back under the blue and white blanket. He was cold.

The following morning the fever stayed away and he began to get well, slowly.

The doctor told him to try to get up and lie in a deck chair on the verandah; the doctor also gave permission to one of the young Dutch officials, a district officer, to visit him and to tell him that the professor had been murdered —he had to know.

Radèn Mas Suprapto was lying in the long rattan chair, amidst the potted palms, in a batik sarong and jacket, a kerchief loosely tied around his head, and he listened to the district officer. The officer was a young man in a white suit, blond, blue eyes—an agreeable-looking fellow. Suprapto had greeted him curtly, 'please sit down, forgive me, I'm not able to get up to greet you,' his face was darker than usual, tight, and he seemed deadly tired, kept closing his eyes.

The officer told him: when the professor had not come home, had not returned after some days, the town had begun to worry and he himself had been sent out with several policemen. First, the road along the outer bay to the Rajah at the tip of the peninsula—that's where the professor had gone, the hotel owner and the doctor had said. He, Suprapto, had been too ill to be asked about it.

'Yes,' Suprapto said, his eyes closed.

The Rajah had been baffled. The professor had been there that day, certainly, just for a short visit. He had accepted only a drink of coconut water and he had bought the flowers and plants the children had collected from him. He had distributed dimes and quarters—they weren't to take all that trouble for nothing, he had said, although his botanical case had been already half filled with wild orchids. He had to go back immediately, his assistant was seriously ill.

The officer stopped for a moment.

Radèn Mas Suprapto remained silent.

The Rajah had wanted to accompany the professor back, but he had refused—'I can go quicker alone,' he had said. But the Rajah together with all the children had escorted him to the edge of the village anyway and the professor had looked around and waved, as he always did, the Rajah had related.

'Yes,' said Suprapto.

So they had taken up the search from there: he, the policemen, the Rajah from the tip of the peninsula, and many others (everyone wanted to help); first along all the roads and paths which enter the mountains from there; they had inquired in the mountain villages, with no result.

'Then back again, the road along the outer bay, you know that it's a long and lonely road, up to the settlement of the Binongkos. I had them all called together, in that one large cabin—'

Suprapto seemed to be asleep.

'Do you remember the settlement of the Binongkos? There is a little roofed bridge across the river there.'

'Yes.'

'One of my policemen is a Binongko, or anyway he speaks their language. We questioned them—nobody knew a thing. In the morning the professor had passed there on his way to the Rajah, a girl had given him flowers, she had done that once before; the professor had paid her two quarters for them, as he had done before—'

'Yes,' Suprapto said again.

In the afternoon the professor had passed on his way back—that was all they knew.

Which way? Just the usual way to town.

He had never arrived in town? They couldn't explain that.

Had anyone talked to him? No one had talked to him.

Had the girl given him flowers? The girl hadn't given him flowers in the afternoon; she had done that in the morning.

The officer paused, then he leaned a little nearer to Suprapto. 'Something happened then—it is difficult to explain it—that large dirty hut full of people, so dark that you could hardly see. And all the way at the back four young men sitting next to each other on a mat on the ground; in the doorway near me the girl of the flowers was standing, a sad little thing, and she looked as if someone had beaten her, hit her on the mouth—her lips were burst and bloody.

'She stood there without saying anything but she kept looking at me and then again at the four men in the back of the hut, and then again at me; and it was as if she were saying it in loud words. I had the four young men get up and step out into the light—at first they refused, they all held machetes—but there were enough policemen there —two of them had cuts on their hands and forearms, not serious.

'But the girl remained standing where she was, and kept looking at me and then again at the mat on which they had been sitting, and again at me. I had the mat lifted up, there was nothing to be seen, but the earth underneath it seemed freshly broken; and there we found buried the watch and chain of the professor, the gold frame of his glasses, his wallet, two bags with a few dimes and quarters left in them, not many.

'After that it was all quickly done with. One of the four young men came out with the whole story and turned witness against the other three—state witness, so to speak!' said the officer and grinned, 'on the bridge, under the roofing—there had been a short struggle: the old man with his plant knife against four machetes. They had used the dull edge to avoid too much blood, afterward they had hurriedly carried him to the beach, robbed him of his belongings, rolled him up in an old mat, bound it with rattan rope and tied a basketful of stones—such as they use for anchoring—to it, loaded him into one of the winged proas, rowed him out into the bay—there was no one there at that time of the afternoon—and they dropped him overboard.

'I asked, was he sure that the professor was dead then? Yes, the man thought the professor had been dead.

'After that I had to go back inside the hut to get the

things which had been buried there, seal them up as evidence. The girl of the flowers was standing there again and kept pointing to her fingers—one two three four—the four quarters which belonged to her, two from the first time, two the second time, you know!'

And Radèn Mas Suprapto said again, 'Yes.'

'I couldn't give them to her, of course; luckily I had four quarters myself, but not such brightly polished ones—she was very disappointed.'

The officer paused, and then he said, 'when I gave her those four quarters I thought that for these she had—well, yes, properly speaking—turned in, informed on four of her own people: a quarter apiece, that is really not much!' He looked at the other from aside, the sick man's face was so yellow and tired, and his eyes still closed. 'I hope my story has not taken too much out of you,' he then said, and stood up.

Radèn Mas Suprapto opened his eyes, regarded him, 'out of me? no,' he said, and after a while, 'I thank you for calling on me.'

They shook hands.

Later, on the verandah in front of the Club, the district officer asked the doctor, 'are you sure? Is that Javanese assistant of the professor really getting well? He doesn't look it to me.'

'He's been very ill,' the doctor said, 'and perhaps he didn't particularly enjoy the story of how the professor was murdered. We didn't enjoy it here, and we hardly knew him; a card game, a story, a drink—the old man liked a drink—and whether we had ever seen a shell or a fish of this or that description.'

One of the other members said, 'and his damned Javanese clerk had to pick that day to get sick!'

When Suprapto had completely recovered, and shortly before he was to return to Java, the district officer came to call on him again one morning. The Binongko, the 'state witness,' was going to point out the place where they had dropped the professor's body into the outer bay. They wanted to find out whether it would be possible to recover the body and send it to Scotland for burial there.

Suprapto hesitated—why should he go along? But he ended by sitting next to the Dutch official under the wooden roofing of the police proa.

A large proa: a steersman, many rowers, two men to do the soundings later, two police guards on a bench with the Binongko between them. He was handcuffed with iron rings around his wrists and a long thin chain between them; his ankles were shackled too, with a shorter, heavier chain.

Suprapto had seated himself in such a way that he did not have to look at him.

The gong and drum players sat on the roof over their heads: the beating of their instruments sounded regular and almost cheerful over the outer bay, at the end of each beat there was one ringing stroke on the gong. Every now and again the rowers accentuated the rhythm by hitting the boards of the boat with their oars, then put them back into the water with a splash and pulled again.

It was still early in the morning.

Suprapto had the feeling of being on his way to where things would be new, as if in the cool of the new day he himself was a new man, no longer burdened by what had been—light, and without ballast!

Without ballast . . .

He shook his shoulders.

It was good to sail in a proa over a murmuring bay, no matter what, under the sound of the drums—why had they never done that before?

'And might even have drowned on the way,' the professor said.

Suprapto started to lift his hands to his ears but he did not get that far.

The coast, low at first, became steeper: loosely piled rust-brown rocks, heavily overgrown, not only with green bushes but also high straight trees; a couple stood apart from the others, flowers all around them, a swarm of copper-green parakeets rose fluttering and screeching.

Trees, trees, how I like . . .

The wind from the outer bay now gained strength, the swell grew heavier, the rowers had difficulty pulling against it and they sighed, swore, and then laughed again.

'Going back we'll have the wind and the current with us,' the steersman promised.

The scorched slope, the river which cut deeply into the coastline and carried its sandy brown water far out into the bay; on the beach, under the trees, the winged proas were gone. The little roofed bridge across the river was invisible from the bay.

The Binongko made a movement as if he wanted to stand up. One of the guards, not the one who spoke his language, the other, said shortly in Malayan, 'sit down, you dog!'

And it was as if the man understood, he ducked with his head.

Suprapto felt a shiver across his back—*dog—dogs* . . . They went on.

Then the Dutch officer said, 'it should be somewhere around here,' and to the guard, 'ask him, will you?'

And the guard who could talk to him asked the Binongko, who was watching the coast attentively and who now pointed with his shackled hand to a tree rising above the others, as if he were drawing a line from tree to proa —'here!' he said.

The guard passed the word to the steersman and he to the drummers, and when the drums stopped the rowers immediately stopped too, let the water run off the oars, took them in and laid them down. All but a few who went on sculling, with the steersman, to keep the bow of the proa on the waves.

Suddenly there was an almost tangible silence.

Only the sound of the surf on the coast, the steady murmur of the ocean far out, and the wind, in gusts.

The two men let out the sounding line over the edge of the proa.

The Binongko stood up (the guards let him); he spoke some words—repeated the same ones, it seemed—no one understood him except the one police guard but he paid no attention. Nobody paid attention.

Nobody listened—but they all looked at him.

The two under the roof, the rowers on each side of the proa; the two with the sounding lead worked on the line but they looked at him too, and so did the guards. All looked, all those pairs of dark eyes and the one pair of blue eyes, all looked at the shackled man standing in their midst—the murderer.

Nobody spoke.

Suprapto had the feeling of circles—concentric circles.

First the murderer: his handcuffs and chains made him seem enclosed and encircled within himself.

Then all of them around the man.

The proa again around them.

Outside—the open—water, waves, coast, trees, wind and sky—were no part of this, could not set them free from the circles. They had no link with all that any more.

No one spoke, no one moved.

Only the line of the lead running farther out; the steersman holding the long oar, two rowers sculling with short ones. But the feeling of a slow encirclement, of a tightening ring, was so strong—the atmosphere so oppressive and threatening—that Suprapto thought he couldn't bear it any longer; did the man next to him feel nothing?

It was then that the district officer got up, looked over the roof, turned his head smartly toward the steersman, called out—steersman!—as has been done at all times when there is danger at sea.

'Steersman, watch it! And remember, no tricks, do you hear?'

The young voice sounded authoritative yet not too emphatic, very clear; everyone in the proa could hear his words but they were directed only to the steersman.

'Aye, sir,' said the steersman and as if the others hadn't heard he repeated (that was his duty), 'men, remember, no tricks, do you hear? the officer says,' and 'the wind is staying nice and steady for the way back!'

'Aye, steersman,' one of the rowers answered for all of them.

And it was over. The tightening circles had been loosened, without much effort.

The Binongko sat down again between his two guards.

The rowers relaxed, stretched, looked at one another, laughed at something, cut a quid of tobacco, smoked, chewed on a nutmeg. 'Come on, you!' someone shouted to the leadsmen.

The policemen lit self-rolled cigarettes. The one—not he who could talk with the murderer, the one who had called him 'dog'—asked the officer whether he (he pointed at the Binongko with his thumb) could have one too.

'It's all right with me,' the officer said.

The Binongko accepted the cigarette and the match—his chain was so light that he could easily lift his hands. He smoked, his face was as before, like brown clay.

The two under the roof smoked too.

'Yes,' the officer said after a while, squinting against the smoke, 'there are things—a man thinks he's doing his duty and yet, I don't know'—and he stared at his cigarette.

'Do you mean to say that we should have thrown that man overboard, chains and all?' Suprapto asked bluntly.

'No,' said the other, 'that's just it, no! But I do understand how the men feel.'

'Yes,' the Javanese said, 'a stranger—they hate strangers.'

'No, no, that's not the reason! Of course they're not particularly fond of these half savages who land on their

islands, burn off whole stretches, exhaust the earth and
then vanish again; no, it's certainly because of the murder.
Perhaps you don't quite understand—they're spirited fellows, there are many soldiers among them, from tradi-
tional soldiering families, they are fighters, not lap dogs—'

Dogs—you and I . . .

'When one man knifes another on account of a woman
or an old feud, or just because he doesn't like him, they
don't mind so much—but four young men with machetes
who set on a myopic old man whom they know to be
unarmed,' and he made a face of disgust.

'Did they know he was unarmed?' the Javanese started
to ask, but he didn't say the words out loud.

And I still have my plant knife, young friend . . .

'And then, the island considered him more or less its
property. Do you know how they called him here? "Mister
only-half-crazy." He had already made a place in their
songs, with his topee and glasses and parasol and that
green plants case and his polished dimes and quarters.
They knew that he didn't do harm to their children,
didn't lure them into the woods or things like that, he
made his watch chime for them, grinned, and if he pushed
beautiful dimes or quarters into their hands for a flower or
a plant instead of pennies—well, if he wanted to be
crazy, others must keep their hands off him! And assassina-
tions aren't their style.'

'Wasn't this more of a hold-up murder?' the Javanese
asked in his clipped voice.

'All right, if you prefer, a hold-up murder,' the officer
said, suddenly annoyed. 'You knew the professor better
than I, but I have the feeling that there aren't so many of

his caliber, even considering all his peculiarities. I tell you, when I think about that bridge and what happened there, and afterward—then I stand with *my* men!' He said it clearly, emphatically, put himself on their side: '*my* men.'

All of them: rowers, steersman, drum players, police, leadsmen, all were *my* men—except the Binongko, not he, and of course not Suprapto, the Javanese, the stranger—curious, wasn't it, that he had to be ill just that day. . . .

He would be silent again, think his answers, his remarks, not say them out loud, and his thoughts became bitter and suspicious again as before, and burned like acid in a wound.

The leadsmen were finished, had taken the line back in, and one of them wrote slowly and solemnly in a notebook.

'How many fathoms?' the officer asked dutifully.

'More than two hundred fathoms,' said the man and put the book away.

'That's deep,' the officer said.

In deep water . . . or we'll grow old . . . you too, Radèn Mas Suprapto . . . like the other prince . . .

The drum players on the roof played a bit, just lightly, for themselves, soft and swift—dook-dooke-dook and the plong of the gong.

Dook-dooke-dook-dook-dooke-dook-plong!

'Is there anything you might want?' the officer asked awkwardly, and the Javanese said, 'no, not I, thank you.'

'Well, we'll go back then, steersman.'

The steersman told the drum players, who stopped. Then a few hard blows on the gong—attention!—the rowers took the oars, dipped them into the water.

And they went back.

The two sat under the roof.

It had become warmer. The sky, at first so dome-high and open and blue, was now hazy, untransparent, white heat vibrations running through it; the water in the outer bay was much wilder, with whitecaps on the gray of the waves, and a growling sea in the distance.

I . . . I'm afraid of the sea, young friend . . .

Suprapto rubbed his forehead—how annoying was that beating of the drums and especially that ringing blow on the gong all the time, right over his head.

After a while the officer said, 'we'll never be able to pull him up, we don't even have diving suits; and the Binongko says "here," but it might as well be somewhere else; anyway, what will be left of him? I'm afraid the professor will have to be satisfied with a watery grave! Did he like the sea?'

'No,' the Javanese answered slowly, 'the professor said that he'—'feared,' he had started to say—'that he didn't like the sea much.'

And then he asked, 'in your job, you must often be at sea, have you ever seen those little jellyfish? "Mizzens" they are called, they can put up some sort of a membrane like a sail.'

The officer laughed, 'what makes you think of that so suddenly? They're quite common in the Sea of Banda, masses of them, they sting like the devil when you touch them. Yes, I've seen them.'

'Would they come here too?' the Javanese asked, and he pointed to the place they had just left behind them.

The officer looked, 'perhaps,' he said, 'I don't know, the

outer bay is quite open there, but they appear only at a certain time of the year, I think. Shall I ask the steersman?'

'No, don't bother,' said the Javanese, and after a while, 'Rumphius says that they're quite beautiful.'

'Yes,' said the officer, 'a strange poisonous green, with long blue streamers, and the sails are sort of transparent with a colored edge.'

'A crystal sail edged with purple or violet.'

'Yes,' the officer agreed, a bit astonished.

'Like a jewel, Rumphius said.'

'Yes,' there was a flicker of enthusiasm in the blue eyes, 'yes, that's true!'

Glorious, someone said.

And Suprapto continued, 'I guess the sails aren't very big—'

'No, how could they be big? Without the streamers these jellyfish aren't big themselves—the sails aren't bigger than —' the officer looked around for something to compare them with: his own firm hand, and then the slim dark hand which the Javanese held on his knee. He didn't touch it, but he pointed at it, his finger moving over the knuckles, 'a bit larger than the width of your hand perhaps.'

Suprapto looked where the other had pointed—his own thin hand.

'Yes,' he said in his even, toneless voice, 'I realized that those sails are small—not big.'

For a short moment it caused him an almost inhuman pain.

· FOUR ·

THE ISLAND

AND SO the lady of the Small Garden wanted to be alone for one day and night of the year.

Early in the morning she had sent all the servants and their families to the town at the outer bay in the milk proa. It became quite a party, they liked to make a trip to town all together, and they would come back the following day.

Sjeba and her husband, Henry, who was still cowherd, stayed with her. Slowly they had become the only ones left from the past, the only ones who knew everything, had gone through everything—anyway, the cows had to be milked.

The day had been dry and sunny, and there would be a full moon in the evening—it didn't always happen that way, often this evening and night had been a pit of darkness for her.

Not this time.

When the moon rose above the inner bay, which lay as quiet as a lake, and shone over the foliage of the trees and palms on the beach, it seemed almost day. The small leaves of the many palms gleamed as if wet, as if the moonlight would roll off them in silver drops and trickles. The trunks of the plane trees lighted up gray and silvery white, the foliage took on a hard, almost metallic gleam.

It was still, there was hardly a murmur from the inner bay; the waves of the surf—the father, the mother, the child—ran out on the beach with a little sigh.

Now the crabs and the lobsters came out of their caves: those with the white gleaming eyes, those whose shells shine in the moonlight like mother-of-pearl. One of the large tree crabs, which were becoming so rare—hard blue with white stripes, Don Diego in full harness, Mr. Rumphius said—climbed into a coco palm, cut off a nut, dropped it on the ground, climbed down, tore off the shell and slowly began to crack the stone-hard nut between its claws. The sound could be heard quite a distance in the night's silence.

The species of lobster with the single, monstrously enlarged claw which was constantly moving up and down would be somewhere near the water, waving at the moon—that's what they did.

The tiny duck crabs with their scarlet legs could safely crawl around while the cruel ducks were asleep.

All the brightly colored little fishes woke up and swam through the moonlit water where it wasn't too deep—fleeting flashes of gold, red, and light blue.

In the deep center of the bay the big fish hid: the robbers with swords and saws and pointed shark's teeth, with the sweeping knife-sharp ray's tails.

Later the fishermen from the village would pass by, wading into the water up to their knees, with torches and bamboo spears to spear the little fish. They were careful to stay out of the moonlight and within the darkness of the coast with its high trees, so as not to throw shadows. In the past the lady of the Small Garden had occasionally gone with them, her sarong bound up and pieces of leather under her feet against the sea urchins, but she had pitied the pretty fishes and been afraid of octopuses.

So were the fishers. A short time ago an octopus had wound itself around the arm of a fisher and had let go only when he held his burning torch against it. The man had burned his arm; he was still coming to the Small Garden for ointment.

The lady of the Small Garden brought out her little rattan chair and put it on the beach near the stone quay which had just been built. The old one with the pieces of white marble had slowly collapsed—now a proa could once again moor decently and her guests wouldn't get their feet wet. She was a hospitable woman and always had many visitors.

That night there would be four, and they would not

need a proa; perhaps they had already arrived. It was different each year, there had been years when no one had come.

But this year there were four: A Scotch professor, a woman from the island whose name was Constance, a sailor from Macassar, and the retired commissioner who had lived at the outer bay.

Two she knew by face: the professor she had met several times in town, with his young Javanese assistant. They had immediately been deep in conversation about their mutual friend, Mr. Rumphius, and the professor had asked her whether she had ever seen a 'mizzen.' She had invited them to the Garden to search for trees and plants and flowers, and she had looked forward to it: she would be able to show them the way—the way to so many things!

She had thought the professor a bit grotesque—weren't professors often? She had never before seen one as they are caricatured, distracted, with umbrellas they are always leaving behind. The professor had a large parasol but he didn't seem distracted. She had liked him very much.

She hadn't known quite what to think of the young Javanese: so refined in appearance, so reserved, not to be reached, and yet overflowing with something—she didn't know what. But what did it matter now?

Constance had been the cook of the official and his wife who lived in her old house in town with their child Sophy. She remembered Constance; she hadn't been a woman one forgets easily. But what was Constance really like? She had had a walk like a queen in exile. The lady of the Small Garden had heard the strange story about the sailor's knife—she always heard all the stories.

She had never seen the sailor; but sailors are usually nice.

The commissioner she had not only never seen, she couldn't visualize him either. If one listened to the stories about him, he really couldn't have been very pleasant. At the auction she had bought the one beautiful jug with the lion heads and the rattan rope (much too expensive!).

Would the three little girls come? The real ones— Elsbet, Katie, Marregie? She didn't know yet; did they belong to it or did they not? But this was their place, and children are curious, she thought.

Perhaps they were all together in the living room; she had put plants and flowers there as usual. She had not burned incense as her grandmother would have done— the congealed tears—tears enough!

Her son—this was the night of her son—did not always come either. Yet he belonged to it, she thought, because this was the day, the night, of the murdered.

She wasn't an oversensitive woman and certainly not sentimental, but she would always keep that deep and burning pity for those who had been murdered; she rebelled against it, murder, she couldn't accept it, not for her son nor for anyone, not then, not now, and not in all eternity.

Dying, yes!—everybody must die, young or old, from sickness, age, an accident, perhaps even from Venom, but then by mistake. One has to resign oneself to that. But it is not good that one human being is killed by another.

And so on that one day and night of the year she

commemorated together with her son all those who had been murdered on the island—that was all she could do for them.

'She never quite got over it,' her friends in the town at the outer bay whispered, 'that's why at times she's a bit—although she is still quite sharp!'

They couldn't say to her, 'you must try and get over it,' that made her furious, 'do you think we should get over each other,' she asked, 'is that what you think?'

'Without love, without loyalty, without memory—cowards!' she would mutter afterward. Cowards, that was it—it hurt them too much.

As she had tasted bitterness, more bitter than the bitter water from the bitter spring, so she now knew pain, inside and outside—and what is there to still pain?

She did not have the firm belief of her grandmother.

There are those who say, see with your eyes, hear with your ears, but know, know without seeing or hearing; none of that was given to her—never, not once—she did not even meet him in a dream any more.

There were the silent conversations but she had no illusions about them. She asked, and she gave his answer to her questions. He was not only her child, he was close to her, and she had begun to know him so well, especially in that last part of his life, that she could put his questions and answer them—but what had all that to do with him?

It was never a communion with him as a being, detached from her, with his own face—at most it was with that small part of him that lay enclosed within herself.

Did he still exist as a being, or was there only his silence? Had she—with that everlasting conversation, the questions and the answers—had she locked out his silence with that?

But she was a woman living on earth who had loved her child living on earth—perhaps it was his silence which she could not bear.

While she was thinking this, looking over the inner bay in the moonlight for the thousandth time, thinking it and not thinking it, she suddenly had the feeling that there was someone sitting with her on the little wooden bench against the plane tree, outside of the moonlight, in the dark. She couldn't see anything, but if there was someone it was not her son Himpies but another: someone she did not know, whom she had never met, someone she did not like, she was certain of that!

The commissioner, she thought, annoyed, who else, why did he come and sit here? At first she remained silent.

'Why don't you go in and join the others?' she asked after a while, 'the professor is very agreeable and the sailor too, I think. Constance is a queer one but she is pleasant to look at, the three girls are nice children, if they're there—' She didn't mention her son, and she received no answer.

It irritated the lady of the Small Garden, she'd rather sit alone at the inner bay—what did he want, did he think he didn't belong inside?

'Well, you were murdered too, weren't you?' she asked then.

'Drowned,' said whoever it was, testily.

'Oh yes,' the lady of the Small Garden said with impatience, 'we know that, but did you drown or did they drown you?'

'I don't know.'

She made such a sudden movement that the old rattan chair creaked in all its joints.

'Nonsense!' she said, 'you must know whether you fell or were pushed.'

'Both, madam,' the commissioner or whoever it was answered seriously and politely.

What can one say to that?

She stood up without looking at him and went toward the house, her house which was really a guest pavilion: four rooms in a row with a side gallery. The moon was now shining in through the pillars. Here she had so often sat with her grandmother, each leaning against a stone pillar—here the bibi had opened her basket and brought out the strings of white shells with the two children watching, Himpies closest—here was the spot, to the left of the third pillar (she could find it with her eyes closed), where she often stood, looking straight ahead: over the flower bed between the nutmeg trees where the house had been (the house that must not be rebuilt) and then farther on, through the valley with the shell of the Leviathan, across the river, the wood, the hills, the sea, the other island, 'the land at the other side,' the high mountains there, straight on to the clearing in the jungle.

Where her son had been murdered by the Mountain Alfura, the warrior who, dark and nude and resplendent in his white loin girdle and his white porcelana shells, stood waiting behind a tree—shot through his unprotected throat while he was catching his breath with his men and Domingoes, talking, laughing at the old convict—

'And yet I wasn't only murdered, mother, I fell in battle, that too.'

How often had he not said that—she thought he would say it that way; she never answered: if that's the way he wanted it—but she knew better.

From where she stood she looked straight at the path—was it a path?—along which they had carried the stretcher all those hours, taking turns at holding the wound closed —in the end only the old man, while her son slowly bled to death under his fingers, and Domingoes walked at his side and looked at him and said, 'oh soul . . .'—or didn't he?

From here she looked straight at his grave on the coast of the island 'at the other side' where the surf came in from the ocean 'with its steadily repeating equally heavy beats,' he had written. She had been there—she could have had him dug up, reinterred, but she did not like digging up. She knew the sound of that surf now.

Here, at this pillar, she talked with him in her fashion.

'Have you been inside?' she asked.

'Yes, mother.'

'How are they?'

'Oh, all right.'

'Are the three girls there?'

'Yes, they too. I especially like the professor.'

'Yes, didn't I tell you?'

'Marregie immediately took possession of him, they were standing at the curiosities cabinet and the professor told her about the shells. I don't think it will be easy for him to get rid of her! But he didn't seem in very good form, something seemed to be bothering him.'

The lady of the Small Garden shrugged.

'Bothering him, indeed! If you've been murdered by a pack of Binongkos—that scum!—murdered and thrown into the sea, perhaps before you are even dead.'

'Yes, no, it isn't always . . .' her son hesitated, groping for the right word; and for one short moment she saw— no! no!—she remembered his face, breath-takingly clear, the eyes with the spots, and it was so close, the way he could look— 'it isn't easy for us human beings to be killed, nor to die in whatever way, mother—'

His face was already gone again.

'No, of course not,' she said, 'but you mustn't mention those two in one breath, you know I can't stand that! Why do you pretend that it's the same, being killed and dying? Because it isn't, and you can't really think that it is.'

'Yes-and-no, mother,' she made her son say, hesitant as he would be—but then her own words angered her and she scolded him, 'don't start with that yes-and-no and one-*and*-the-other, I hate that talk without finality, you should know that by now.'

'Yes, but certainly, Mrs. Small Garden,' her son said without laughing or looking at her, 'but where were we —with the professor; he was telling Marregie the Cinderella story, but a bit differently, all about the double Venus-heart and the Amoret Harp and the Nautilus and the post horn—"see that! You have to blow the post horn!" Marregie called to the other girls, but Elsbet and Katie weren't listening, they were too busy playing with the sailor, with a rope. He must have been showing them how to make sailors' knots.

' "Did you ever sail in a proa?" ' the sailor asked them.

' "Yes, of course."

' "With whom?"

' "The fishermen from the village, and our nurse."

' "A nice nurse?"

'They looked at each other, "Yes, very nice."

' "Where did you go sailing?"

' "Well, here in the inner bay, where else?"

' "Do you know how you have to whistle for the wind, and that you must call him Mister?"

'Elsbet and Katie knew quite well that the Wind had to be called Mister—come here, Mister Wind, loosen your long hair!—and they knew how to whistle for him, they started right in and got louder and louder.

' "Sssh, watch out!" said the sailor, "the others will hear us and you'll wake up the Storm, who's called Baratdaja!"

' "But we like the storm who's called Baratdaja!" the two girls said.

' "Me too!" said the sailor—and they all three started to giggle.

'And then Constance stood up and clapped her hands as they do at the rattan tug-of-war, and started to sing.'

'What did she sing?' the lady of the Small Garden asked her son.

'The song—the drum calls from afar, afar, and—the rattan is broken, we are holding the pieces—it sounded rather sad, I must say.'

'Yes,' the lady of the Small Garden said pensively, 'I imagine so—did she dance too?'

'If you can call it dancing—a few steps forward, a few steps back, and clapping her hands.'

'Did you watch her?'

'Yes,' her son answered, 'yes, the professor and the sailor and I—'

'I would have expected you to watch her,' the lady of the Small Garden answered, and then she said what she had been meaning to say all that time, 'do you know what, that commissioner is sitting all alone on the beach, under the plane trees—it's most annoying, he doesn't want to admit that he was murdered!'

Her son answered, 'but none of us likes to admit that! I've tried so often to explain it to you, can't you listen just once: we're never just murdered, we're always "killed in action" too—don't get angry now, because that's the way it is, one *and* the other, my sweet mother!' He had never called her that.

'Well, that's what the commissioner seems to think too. When I said, "but you must know whether you fell or whether you were pushed," do you know what he answered? "Both, madam," how do you like that!'

Then her son laughed.

She had made him say and ask and answer so many things; he had been sad at times when they talked about Toinette and the child Netty; she couldn't tell him where they had gone. But why had she never made him laugh? Not once—he who had been gay, who liked to laugh, had been laughing when the arrow came, Domingoes had said—this was the first time.

'I think I like the commissioner,' he added.

'No,' the lady of the Small Garden answered in her decisive manner, 'no, he is not agreeable. Come along and find out for yourself.'

She turned around and slowly went back through the side gallery to the garden, she kept to the wall to leave room for someone beside her, down the stairs to the beach, and sat down in her chair.

She sat still in her chair, she had been sitting there all the time.

She had the feeling that the commissioner was no longer there under the plane tree, nor the others inside, not the professor, nor Constance, nor the sailor, nor the three girls—none of them, not her son either.

They had never been there.

'Stay with me,' she suddenly whispered, frightened; closed her eyes for a moment, opened them and then looked silently out again over the inner bay.

The moon threw a path of light over the water, one could have walked on it—the inner bay did murmur now, softly, and the waves of the surf flowed right up to her feet; the large trees stood dark and silent around and behind her. The fishers whom she had seen pass earlier came back, walking in the water: torch in the left hand, spear in the right, to catch the fish when they jumped at the torchlight. They walked carefully in order not to make more noise than the water, they did not talk. But when they saw her sitting in the moonlight, the one whose burned arm she had treated for so long called a greeting to her over the murmur, something like 'good luck to you, madam!'

'Quiet!' the others said, because of the fish—and she

answered back over the water, as softly as possible, 'are you doing well? Yes?' Luck, where is it, that luck?

For the first time that night she came to think of the others, of the murderers—why?

The Mountain Alfura behind the tree.

The four Binongkos of the professor.

The man who had murdered Constance.

The murderer of the sailor, no one knew whether it had been a man or a woman.

The young half-Chinese wife of the commissioner, with her three aunts—or not?

And the Balinese slave girl, the nurse of the three children—who had been so beautiful, who couldn't walk any more afterward—she didn't want to think of her, it was too long ago, and she wasn't allowed to, her grandmother had forbidden her to think of it.

The mass-murderer who had wanted to save her son.

She pressed the tips of the fingers of one hand against her forehead just above the eyebrows—how many murderers there were! It made her dizzy, and at the same time she was astonished about something: while thinking of them she did not feel the anger, the disgust of always, but pity almost; not the large and burning pity that came for those who were murdered, but a small feeling of impatience, of sadness—oh why, why, you fools!—without the desire for revenge, without hatred now. As if they were not the murderers but also among the murdered.

And then there were no more murderers and murdered.

It was so hazy, it all ran together in her head; after all it was one-*and*-the-other, as her son wanted it.

She took her hand away, shook her head, shifted in her

chair: she liked her t's crossed—this *or* that—and no nonsense. Were the t's ever crossed, was anything ever completed? She looked up and then she saw—did she *see?*—in the empty path of light over the water of the inner bay, far away and near, moving and wholly motionless . . .

The purple Palm of the Sea, and under it her grandmother and Mr. Rumphius and the coral woman in her flowery dress; her grandmother held the poison plate from Ceram and put the sentinels of Good Fortune in it which she picked from the Palm; between its roots sat the Crab which controls the tides, and up in the branches the holy Bird had its nest.

The stranger from the hotel whom she had loved—and loved now, and always—held the stolen snake with the Carbuncle Stone in his hand, she would have given it to him if he had asked for it, free as a gift for nothing to keep—the bitter water from the bitter spring flowed over his feet.

The bibi of whom she had been afraid showed her basket to the three pink girls; all the pearls of the commissioner were in it, pearls of the sea, and the other string of beads, fading orange and yellow, pearls from the earth, and strings and strings of gleaming white porcelana shells of Mountain Alfuras in war dress—they couldn't do any harm now.

Her sweet son was standing beside a woman, Toinette and a daughter Netty, they had their backs turned toward her (that was her own fault), they were watching a fleet sail up the inner bay, a fleet of a thousand sails all together, crystal mizzens with edges of purple and violet—

they weren't large, nor small, they reached to the sky, where was the professor now?

Her father and mother with the five Pekingese on leashes.

The four visitors of that evening: the professor—there he was—Constance and her sailor, the commissioner, she now saw all four faces clearly—she would have liked to wave at the professor but she wasn't supposed to, she could only look.

All the murderers, because they had to be there too.

The most beautiful shells: in the middle two enormous crenated shells against each other, the Leviathan from her youth who is too terrible lived in them again, and the smallest of the smallest shells in the world next to him, the gleaming little 'white lice' of which the professor had told Marregie that evening; also the double Venus-heart which is very rare, also the Amoret Harp which her son had held to his ear to listen to.

The white stone from the 'special drawer' with its child— three young men, Bear, Domingoes and Martin the Portuguese seaman who had drowned long ago—the child Sophy with the tame cockatoo she had given her, Sophy's nurse who was herself a child—a young Javanese was drawing a proa on the waves and his name was Radèn Mas Suprapto; a very slender Javanese lady in a coach-man's cape watched him, 'you've forgotten the ballast again,' she said—who was she? the lady of the Small Garden didn't know her, what did she mean by that? The Binongko girl of the flowers sucked on her bleeding lip and listened; from the Portuguese wharf on the other side came the sound of hammering—and the three little girls, the real ones, were standing side by side, they held the snakestone, the knife of the sailor, and Marregie blew on the post horn—coral, fishes, crabs, the three young turtles—the Dancer with the Shell—birds, butterflies.

The stork, the bird lakh-lakh with his long bill and fiery red legs, and the roaring lions, in between them the boy Himpies was sitting on his mat and looking around with large enraptured eyes, and everywhere the small silver waves; and slowly, with long pauses, a voice said from far away, the bay, the inner bay—will you ever forget the inner bay, oh soul of—?

What was happening to her, was she dying, were those her 'hundred things'?

She sat quietly in her chair, they weren't a hundred things but much more than a hundred, and not only hers; a hundred times 'a hundred things,' next to each other, separate from each other, touching, here and there flowing into each other, without any link anywhere, and at the same time linked forever . . .

A link which she did not quite understand; understanding it was not needed, wasn't possible, she had seen it—for one moment over the moonlit water.

She hadn't noticed Sjeba and her husband Henry the cowherd who had come around the house and were now standing to the left and right of her chair.

'Why don't you come to bed?' Sjeba asked, grumbling and at the same time worried, and they both shook their heads, 'why are you sitting here? The moon is shining, but what good does that do, it only makes one sick! There's fresh coffee in the kitchen, and you'd better come inside now.'

Then the lady of the Small Garden whose name was Felicia stood up from her chair obediently and without looking around at the inner bay in the moonlight—it would remain there, always—she went with them, under the trees and indoors, to drink her cup of coffee and try again to go on living.

About the Author

Maria Dermoût was born in 1888 in Java, then part of
the Dutch East Indies. She was educated in Holland,
and returned to the Indies in 1905, living there for the
next thirty years with her husband, a jurist. She died in
Holland in 1961. *The Ten Thousand Things* was
first published in 1955, and enjoyed great
international success.